MW01088199

TREASURE ISLAND

A Kaplan Vocabulary-Building Classic for Young Readers

ROBERT LOUIS STEVENSON

Get Wild About Reading!
Enjoy your book!
Compliments of:
The RJO-PFO and
The PARP Committee

**Look for more
Kaplan Vocabulary-Building Classics
for Young Readers**

Great Expectations
by Charles Dickens

The Adventures of Tom Sawyer
by Mark Twain

Little Women
by Louisa May Alcott

TREASURE ISLAND

A Kaplan Vocabulary-Building Classic for Young Readers

ROBERT LOUIS STEVENSON

ABRIDGED

SIMON & SCHUSTER
NEW YORK LONDON SYDNEY TORONTO

Kaplan Publishing
Published by SIMON & SCHUSTER
Rockefeller Center
1230 Avenue of the Americas
New York, NY 10020

Editorial Director: Jennifer Farthing
Project Editor: Cynthia C. Yazbek
Content Manager: Patrick Kennedy
Abridgement and Adaptation: Caroline Leavitt for Ivy Gate Books
Interior Design: Ismail Soyugenc for Ivy Gate Books
Cover Design: Mark Weaver

Manufactured in the United States of America
Published simultaneously in Canada

10 9 8 7 6 5 4 3 2 1

April 2006
ISBN-13: 978-0-7432-8105-8
ISBN-10:   0-7432-8105-5

For information regarding special discounts for bulk purchases, please
contact Simon & Schuster Special Sales at 1-800-456-6798 or
business@simonandschuster.com.

TABLE OF CONTENTS

HOW TO USE THIS BOOK

Robert Louis Stevenson's *Treasure Island* is a classic tale of adventure. It also is a way for today's young people to enrich their vocabularies – for tests as well as for daily writing and speaking.

Kaplan makes it as easy for you to learn dozens – even hundreds – of new words just by reading this classic story. On the right-hand pages you will find the words of Stevenson's famous novel. Some of these words have been bolded (put into heavy, dark type). These are words found on tests you take, both for specific subjects and for standardized tests. On the left-hand pages you'll find information about those words: how to pronounce them, what part of speech they are, what they mean, and even what synonyms they have. In short, you'll find everything you will need to master each of these special words in the story.

Not all of the challenging or unusual words in *Treasure Island* are usually found on tests. Some are words that were used most often in Stevenson's day, 125 years ago and more. You might want to learn these words as well, even though they are not likely to appear on tests you take. For this reason we have underlined them and put information about them in the glossary at the back of this book.

You'll also find other helpful features in this book. "Robert Louis Stevenson" provides useful information about Stevenson's life and his books, which will help you enjoy your reading even more. The back of the book also contains a section that will assist you in writing a book report about *Treasure Island*. Use it to develop and order your thoughts and ideas about the book.

You will also find some discussion questions. These will get you thinking about the characters, events, and meaning of this classic novel. They will also help you get ready to discuss it in class, with friends, or even with your family members.

Now it's time to get started reading one of the most famous classics of all time.

ROBERT LOUIS STEVENSON

Born in Edinburgh, Scotland, in 1850, Robert Louis Stevenson came from a family of engineers. He chose law as a profession, however, and entered the University of Edinburgh.

Beginning in his teens, he began to write, and by the time he was in his early twenties, he was an accomplished writer of travel literature. His journeys, however, were brought about more by a quest for good health than by curiosity of faraway places. Stevenson was troubled by ill health, especially by weak lungs, and he searched for a climate that would improve his condition.

During his lifetime, Stevenson wrote a number of books that have become classics such as *Treasure Island* (written in 1883), *Kidnapped* (1886), *The Black Arrow* (1888), and *The Master of Ballantrae* (1889).

Afflicted with a severe case of tuberculosis, he failed to find a place where his lungs could get the fresh air he needed. He died, in Samoa, in 1894, at the age of forty-four.

A Scale of 3 English Miles

Foremast Hill

North Inlet

Strong tide here

Spyglass Hill

Rifol Cove

Swamp

Swamp

Cape of ye Woods

Skeleton Island

Mizenmast Hill

Hautbowline Head

Seal Ground

TREASURE ISLAND

Augt 1750. W B

Given by above J. F. & Mr W. Bones Maste of ye Walrus

Savannah this twenty July 1754 W B

Facsimile of Chart, latitude and

longitude struck out by J Hawkins

TREASURE ISLAND

LOCATION (lo <u>kay</u> shun) *n.*
the place where something is
Synonyms: position, direction

LODGING (<u>loj</u> ing) *n.*
a place where someone lives or stays, usually
only a short time
Synonyms: dwelling, housing

SOILED (soyld) *adj.*
covered with dirt
Synonyms: filthy, dirty, unclean

CHAPTER 1

I have been asked to write the whole story of Treasure Island, telling everything but the **location** of the island, because there is still treasure there. I take up my pen and go back to the time when my father kept the <u>Admiral</u> Benbow Inn. That was when the old seaman first took up his **lodging** under our roof.

He first came to the inn door, dragging his sea chest behind him. He was a tall, strong, heavy, nut-brown man. A pigtail fell over the shoulder of his **soiled** blue coat, and a cut from a <u>saber</u> went

PARLOR (<u>par</u> lor) *n.*
a room used for sitting and entertaining
Synonyms: living room, sitting room

HAUNT (hawnt) *v.* **-ing**, **-ed**
to stay on one's mind in a disturbing way
Synonyms: scare, torment

across one cheek. He broke out into a sea-song. "Fifteen men on the dead man's chest – Yo-ho-ho, and a bottle of rum!"

"This is a handy cove," says he, "Do you get much company, mate?"

My father told him no, very little company.

"Well, then," said he, "this is the place for me."

He was a very silent man. All day he hung round the cove or upon the cliffs with a brass <u>telescope</u>. All evening, he sat in a corner of the **parlor** next to the fire. He would not speak when spoken to but would look up sudden and fierce, and we learned to let him be. Every day when he came back from his walk, he would ask if any sailors had gone by along the road. At first we thought he wanted company of men like himself, then we saw that he wanted to avoid them.

One day, he took me aside and promised me a silver <u>fourpenny</u> on the first of every month if I would keep my eye open for a sailor with one leg and let him know the moment he appeared.

That one-legged man **haunted** my dreams.

NIGHTMARE (<u>nite</u> mair) *n.*
a dream that makes one very frightened
Synonyms: bad dream, vision

TERRIFIED (<u>ter</u> uh fyed) *adj.*
filled with fear
Synonyms: afraid, scared

On stormy nights, I would see him leap and chase me, and it was the worst of **nightmares**.

But though I was **terrified** by the idea of the man with one leg, I was less afraid of the captain than were the other people who came to the inn. His stories about hanging and walking the <u>plank</u> frightened everyone. He had lived among some of the wickedest men ever, and the language in which he told these stories shocked all of us.

He stayed with us until all the money he had was gone. If ever my sick father mentioned the money, the captain stared my father out of the room. All the time he lived with us the captain never wrote or received a letter, and he never really spoke with anyone but the neighbors. None of us saw his great sea chest ever opened.

It was not very long after this that my father began to get sicker and sicker, and we began to worry more and more that he might die. One January morning, my mother was upstairs taking care of him, and I was setting the breakfast-table. The captain was down at the beach, his brass telescope under his arm.

MOTION (<u>mo</u> shuhn) *v.* **-ing, -ed**
to direct someone with a movement of the
hand or head
Synonyms: signal, gesture

EXPRESSION (eks <u>spresh</u> uhn) *n.*
the look on someone's face that shows what he
or she feels or thinks
Synonyms: look, appearance

Suddenly the door opened, and a man stepped in. I always had my eye open for sailors with one leg or two, but I wasn't sure about this man. I couldn't tell if he was a sailor or not.

He sat down at a table and **motioned** me to draw near. I stopped where I was, and I saw that he was missing two fingers.

"Is this table for my mate Bill?" he asked.

I told him I did not know his mate Bill and that this was for a person who stayed in our house whom we called the captain.

"My mate Bill would be called the captain," he said. "He has a cut on one cheek. Is he here?"

I told him he was out walking.

"Which way, sonny? Which way is he gone?"

I pointed towards the rocks. "Ah," said he. The **expression** on his face was not pleasant. The stranger patted me on the shoulder and told me I was a good boy. Then he looked out the window and back at me. "And here, coming toward us, is my mate Bill. You and me'll just go back into the parlor, sonny, and get behind the door, and we'll give Bill a surprise."

OATH (ohth) *n.*
nasty or foul language, a swear word
Synonyms: curse, profanity

The stranger took me into the parlor and put me behind him in the corner so that we were both hidden by the open door. I was alarmed, and it made me more scared to see how the stranger was certainly frightened himself. He loosened his knife in the <u>sheath</u>, and he kept swallowing, as if he had a lump in his throat.

At last, the captain came inside the house and marched across the room to his breakfast.

"Bill," said the stranger.

The captain spun around on his heel. He looked like he had seen a ghost.

"Black Dog!" said he.

"I've come to see my old shipmate," he said.

"What do you want?" asked the captain.

They sat on either side of the table. The captain told me to go, and I went into another room.

For a long time, though I certainly did my best to listen, I could hear nothing. But at last I could pick up a word or two, mostly **oaths**, from the captain.

"No, no, no, no!" he cried once.

Then, all of a sudden, the table went over in

FUGITIVE (<u>fyoo</u> juh tiv) *n.*
> someone who runs away, usually from the
> police or other authorities
>> Synonyms: runaway, outlaw

REEL (reel) *v.* **-ing, -ed**
> to walk, moving from side to side, as if one is
> going to fall
>> Synonyms: stumble, sway

FETCH (fech) *v.* **-ing, -ed**
> to go after something and bring it back
>> Synonyms: retrieve, bring

a lump, and there was a clash of steel and then a cry of pain. In the next instant, I saw Black Dog in full flight, and the captain hotly running after him, both with drawn <u>cutlasses</u>. Black Dog had blood streaming from his shoulder. Just at the door the captain aimed at the **fugitive** one last cut.

Once out upon the road, Black Dog disappeared over the edge of the road. The captain turned back into the house. He **reeled** a little and caught himself with one hand against the wall.

"Are you hurt?" cried I.

"I must get away from here!" he cried.

I ran to **fetch** him water. I heard a loud fall in the parlor, and running in I saw the captain lying full length upon the floor. At the same instant, my mother, alarmed by the cries and fighting, came running downstairs to help me. Between us, we raised his head. He was breathing very hard, but his eyes were closed and his face was a horrible color.

We had no idea what to do to help. It was a happy relief for us when the door opened and Doctor Livesey came in on his visit to my sick

STROKE (stroke) *n.*
> a sudden attack caused when blood stops
> flowing to the brain
> > Synonym: apoplexy

RELIEVED (ri <u>leevd</u>) *adj.*
> to have something taken away, usually fear or
> worry
> > Synonym: comforted

HOIST (hoist) *v.* **-ing**, **-ed**
> to pull up with difficulty
> > Synonyms: lift, heave

father. He bent and looked at the captain. "The man has had a **stroke**." the doctor said. "Get me a bowl."

When I got back with the bowl, the doctor had already loosened the captain's shirt and rolled up his sleeve. His great arm was <u>tattooed</u> in several places. After a while, the captain began to look about. First he recognized the doctor. Then his glance fell upon me, and he looked **relieved**. But suddenly his color changed, and he tried to raise himself, crying, "Where's Black Dog?"

"There is no Black Dog here," said the doctor, "You have had a stroke. I'll help you to your bed."

Between us, with much trouble, we managed to **hoist** him upstairs and laid him on his bed, where his head fell back on the pillow.

And with that, the doctor went off to see my father, taking me with him by the arm.

"He should lie for a week where he is," the doctor said, as soon as he had closed the door. "Another stroke would kill him."

Later that day, I brought the captain some cooling drinks and medicine. He was lying much

SUMMONS (<u>suhm</u> uhns) *n.*
a request or a call to take some action
Synonyms: order, warrant, writ

DISTRESS (diss <u>tress</u>) *n.*
a feeling of extreme pain or sadness
Synonyms: pain, heartache, anguish

as we had left him, and he seemed weak and excited.

"Jim," he said, "you're the only one here that's worth anything. Did that doctor say how long I was to lie here?"

"A week at least," said I.

"Thunder!" he cried. "A week! I can't do that. They'll have the black spot on me by then. Listen, you saw that sailor today?"

"Black Dog?"

"He's a bad man, but I tell you, there are worse. They all want my sea chest. If you see the black spot—"

"But what is the black spot, captain?" I asked.

"That's a **summons**, mate. Keep your eye open!"

His voice grew weaker, and soon after I had given him his medicine, he fell at last into a heavy, sleep. I left him to go about my own business.

My father died suddenly that evening. Next morning, the captain came downstairs. But our natural **distress** over my father's death, the visits of

FUNERAL (<u>fyoo</u> nuh ruhl) *n.*
a formal ceremony held when someone dies
Synonyms: services, rites, burial

DREADFUL (<u>dred</u> fuhl) *adj.*
causing feelings of fear
Synonyms: horrible, terrible, scary

COVE (kovel) *n.*
an area of water that stretches past the shoreline
Synonyms: bay, inlet

the neighbors, the **funeral**, and all the work of the inn kept me so busy that I had no time to think of the captain, far less to be afraid of him.

So things passed until the day after my father's funeral. About three o'clock on that cold afternoon, I was standing inside the inn, full of sad thoughts about my father, when I saw someone drawing slowly near. He was blind. He tapped before him with a stick and wore a great green shade over his eyes and nose. He was bent over. I never saw in my life a more **dreadful**-looking figure. He stopped a little ways from the inn, and raising his voice in an odd sing-song, he addressed the air in front of him, "Will any kind friend tell a poor blind man where he is?"

"You are at the Admiral Benbow, Black Hill **Cove**, my good man," said I.

"I hear a voice," said he, "a young voice. Will you give me your hand and lead me in?"

I held out my hand, and he gripped it like a <u>vise</u>. I struggled to pull free, but the blind man pulled me closer. "Now, boy," he said, "take me in to the captain."

WRENCH (rench) *n.*
a sudden, forceful turn causing injury or pain
Synonyms: twist, strain

DAZED (dayzd) *adj.*
very confused, unable to think clearly
Synonyms: stunned, stupefied

MORTAL (mor tuhl) *adj.*
1. causing death, being near to death
   Synonyms: deadly, fatal
2. very great
   Synonym: intense

"Sir," said I, "upon my word I dare not."

"Take me in, or I'll break your arm!" he cried. And he gave it, as he spoke, a **wrench** that made me cry out.

"Come, now, march," he said, and I never heard a voice so cruel and cold and ugly as that blind man's. I began to obey him at once, walking straight in at the door and towards the parlor, where I knew our sick old <u>buccaneer</u> was sitting, **dazed** with rum. The blind man clung to me. "Lead me to him, and when I'm in view, cry out, 'Here's a friend for you, Bill.' If you don't, I'll hurt you!"

I forgot my terror of the captain as I opened the door and cried out the words he had ordered in a trembling voice.

The captain raised his eyes. There was an expression of **mortal** sickness on his face.

"Now, Bill, sit where you are," said the beggar. "Hold out your left hand. Boy, take his left hand by the wrist and bring it near to my right."

We both obeyed, and I saw him pass something from the hollow of his hand into

VANISH (<u>van</u> ish) *v.* **-ing**, **-ed**
to go completely from sight
Synonyms: disappear, evaporate, become
invisible

PECULIAR (puh <u>kyoo</u> lyur) *adj.*
being odd or different
Synonyms: strange, unusual, unique

HASTE (<u>hayst</u>) *n.*
quickness in moving
Synonyms: speed, rapidity, expeditiousness

VAIN (vayn) *n.*
an unsuccessful try or attempt
Synonyms: useless, worthless, failed

SORROW (<u>so</u> roh) *n.*
a feeling of great sadness or grief
Synonyms: heartbreak, misery

the palm of the captain's, which closed upon it instantly.

"And now that's done," said the blind man, and he suddenly let go of me and **vanished** into the road.

The captain looked sharply into his palm.

"Ten o'clock!" he cried. "Six hours left before something happens! We'll have to get them before they get us!" Then he sprang to his feet. He reeled and then, with a **peculiar** sound, fell to the floor.

I ran to him at once, calling to my mother. But my **haste** was all in **vain**. The captain was dead! I had never liked the man, though I had begun to pity him, but as soon as I saw that he was dead, I burst into a flood of tears. It was the second death I had known, and the **sorrow** of the first was still fresh in my heart.

INCLINE (in <u>kline</u>) *v.* **-ing**, **-ed**
    to tend to do something
        Synonyms: favor, gravitate toward

PAYMENT (<u>pay</u> ment) *n.*
    the act of paying or being paid, the amount to
    be paid
        Synonyms: fee, reckoning, sum

CHAPTER 2

I told my mother all that I knew, and we saw ourselves at once in a difficult and dangerous position. Some of the man's money, if he had any left, was certainly due to us. But it was not likely that our captain's shipmates, Black Dog and the blind beggar, would be **inclined** to give up their <u>booty</u> in **payment** of the dead man's debts. Indeed, it seemed impossible for us to remain much longer in the house. We decided to go seek help in the next town. We ran out at once into the fog.

It was already candle light when we reached

COMRADE (<u>kom</u> rad) *n.*
a friend
Synonyms: associate, colleague

ASSISTANCE (uh <u>siss</u> tens) *n.*
help
Synonyms: service, reinforcement

the town, but no person would return with us to the Admiral Benbow. They knew our captain by name – Captain Flint – and that name made them scared. For that matter, anyone who was a **comrade** of the captain's was enough to frighten them to death. In the end, all anyone would do was to give me a loaded <u>pistol</u> and promise to have horses ready in case we were chased on our return. One lad was to ride forward to Doctor Livesey's in search of armed **assistance**.

My heart was beating when we set off for home again. Finally we were home, and the door of the Admiral Benbow closed behind us.

I slipped the lock at once, and we stood and panted for a moment in the dark, alone in the house with the dead captain's body.

On the floor close to his hand there was a little round of paper, blackened on the one side. I could not doubt that this was the *Black Spot*. Taking it up, I found written on the other side, this short message: "You have until ten tonight."

Our old clock began striking. This sudden

DESPAIR (dih <u>spair</u>) *v.* **-ing**, **-ed**
   to lose all hope
      Synonyms: give up, be despondent

ROGUE (rogh) *n.*
   a dishonest person who has no principles
      Synonyms: bandit, lowlife, criminal

noise startled us, but the news was good, for it was only six o'clock.

"Now, Jim," she said, "that key."

I felt in his pockets, but there was no key, and I began to **despair**. Then, I tore open his shirt at the neck, and there, hanging to a bit of string, was the key. We hurried upstairs to the little room where his box stood.

"Give me the key," said my mother. She threw back the lid as fast as she could.

A strong smell of tobacco rose from the inside. There was a tin, some tobacco, a piece of a silver bar, and an old Spanish watch.

Finally, there lay before us the last things in the chest. There was a bundle of papers tied up in oilcloth, and a bag of gold.

"I'll show these **rogues** that I'm an honest woman," said my mother. "I'll take what's owed me and nothing more."

It took a long time to count the money, for the coins were of all countries and sizes, doubloons, and guineas, and pieces of eight, all shaken together. When we were about half-way

WRETCHED (<u>rech</u> id) *adj.*
    extremely unhappy or unfortunate
        Synonyms: miserable, hapless

CEASE (sees) *v.* **-ing, -ed**
    to come to an end
        Synonyms: stop, quit

EARSHOT (<u>eer</u> shot) *n.*
    the range within which a sound may be heard
        Synonym: hearing distance, close range

through, I suddenly put my hand upon her arm, for I had heard a sound that brought my heart into my mouth. It was the tap-tapping of the blind man's cane! It drew nearer while we sat holding our breath. Then it struck sharp on the inn door, and then we could hear the handle being turned and the lock rattling as the **wretched** being tried to enter. At last the tapping died slowly away again until it **ceased** to be heard.

My mother grabbed the gold, and I picked up the oilskin packet, and we ran out of the inn. We heard footsteps, and as we looked back in their direction, we saw the light of a lantern shining towards us.

This was certainly the end for us, I thought. We ran faster. We were just at the little bridge. I helped my mother to the edge of the bank before she could move no further. So there we had to stay, both of us within **earshot** of the inn.

Suddenly, our enemies began to arrive at the door of our inn, the blind beggar with them. "Down with the door!" he cried.

There was a pause, then a cry of

PROMPTLY (<u>prompt</u> lee) *adv.*
>without delay
>>Synonyms: immediately, rapidly

CURSE (kurs) *v.* **-ing**, **-ed**
>to say a bad or impolite word
>>Synonyms: swear, blaspheme

surprise, and then a voice shouting from the house, "Bill's dead!"

"Search him and get the chest," he cried.

I could hear their feet rattling up our old stairs. **Promptly** afterwards, a man leaned out into the moonlight and addressed the blind beggar on the road below him.

"Pew," he cried, "they've been before us. Someone's opened the chest."

"Is it there?" roared Pew.

"The money's there."

"Not the money!" the blind man **cursed**. "Is it on Bill?"

"Nothing on Bill!" he said.

"What are they looking for?" I whispered to my mother, who shook her head.

"It's these people of the inn who took it! It's that boy!" cried Pew. "They must have taken it! I wish I had put his eyes out! Let's find them!"

Then the men came into our old inn, their heavy feet pounding to and fro, as they threw our furniture over and kicked in our doors. Then the men came out, one after another, on the road and said

DESERT (duh <u>sert</u>) *v.* **-ing**, **-ed**
to leave without planning to return
Synonyms: abandon, flee

PANIC (<u>pan</u> ik) *n.*
a sudden, overwhelming fear
Synonyms: alarm, terror, hysteria

REVENGE (ri <u>venj</u>) *n*
harm done to a person as a punishment to
retaliate for harm done to the person seeking
retribution or to someone close to them, such
as a family member
Synonym: counterblow

that we were nowhere to be found. And then there was a loud whistle, twice repeated. I had thought it to be the blind man summoning his crew, but I now saw how the pirates began to stand at attention and look around them. That signal must be warning them of approaching danger!

"There's Dirk again," said one. "Twice! We had better be careful, mates."

"They must be close by," cried Pew. "Scatter and look for them, dogs! Oh, if I had eyes! You have your hands on thousands of gold pieces, you fools, and you stand there! There wasn't one of you dared face Bill, and I did it! And I'm a blind man! And I'm to lose my chance because you won't look harder! Without that money, I'll be a poor beggar. With it, I might be riding in a coach!"

Then another sound came, the tramp of horses galloping. Almost at the same time a pistol shot rang out. The buccaneers turned at once and ran in every direction, and soon there wasn't a sign of them. They had **deserted** Pew, whether in **panic** or out of **revenge** for his angry words to them, I could not tell. He was tapping up and down the road in

FRENZY (<u>fren</u> zee) *n.*
uncontrolled behavior that can be violent
Synonym: fit

DITCH (ditch) *n.*
a narrow channel dug in the ground for
collecting or moving water
Synonym: trench

TRAMPLE (<u>tram</u> puhled) *v.* **-ing, -ed**
to walk or tread heavily
Synonyms: stomp, crush

SUPERVISOR (<u>soop</u> ur vye zur) *n.*
someone in charge
Synonyms: boss, manager

a **frenzy**, calling for his comrades. Finally he took a wrong turn and ran a few steps past me, crying, "Johnny, Black Dog, Dirk," and other names, "You won't leave old Pew!"

Just then the noise of horses grew even louder, and four or five riders came in sight in the moonlight and swept at full gallop down the hill toward Pew.

At this, Pew saw his mistake, and he turned away from the sound of the horses with a scream. He ran straight for the **ditch**, rolling into it. But he was on his feet again in a second and made another dash, right under the horses!

The rider tried to save him but could not. Down went Pew with a cry, and the four hoofs **trampled** him until he moved no more.

I leaped to my feet and called the riders. They were pulling up, horrified at the accident.

Pew was dead. In the meantime, one man rode on, as fast as he could, to tell Doctor Livesey. Another man, the **supervisor** of the group, came back with us to the Admiral Benbow, and you cannot imagine a house in such a state. The clock

SCROLL (skrohl) *n.*

a rolled piece of paper with something written
or drawn on it

Synonym: document

MAGISTRATE (<u>maj</u> uh strate) *n.*

a government official who enforces the law

Synonyms: judge, justice

had been thrown down by these fellows in their hunt after my mother and myself. Though nothing had actually been taken away except the captain's money-bag and a little silver, we were ruined.

"They got the money?" asked the supervisor. "But what were they really after? More money?"

"No, sir. Not money," replied I. "I have a **scroll** in my pocket, and I should like to get it put away safely. Perhaps bring it to Dr. Livesey."

"Perfectly right," he said. "Livesey's a gentleman and a **magistrate**. I'll take you there."

I thanked him, and we soon struck out for Dr. Livesey's house. We rode hard all the way till we drew up before Dr. Livesey's door. We found Dr. Livesey sitting by a bright fire, along with Squire Trelawney.

The supervisor told his story to Dr. Livesey. "And so, Jim," said the doctor, "you have the thing that they were after, have you?"

I gave him the oilskin packet and the doctor put it quietly in his pocket.

The supervisor soon left, and the doctor told me I could sleep at his house that night.

CLUE (kloo) *n.*

a sign or piece of information that helps one
find the answer to a problem or a mystery
Synonyms: hint, lead

CHAPTER 3

"And now, squire," said the doctor. "You have heard of this Flint, I suppose?"

"Heard of him!" cried the squire. "He was the <u>bloodthirstiest</u> buccaneer that sailed."

"And he must have had some treasure!" said the doctor. "Maybe what I have here in my pocket is some **clue** about where Flint buried his treasure! Do you think that treasure might amount to much?"

"It will amount to a fortune! If we have the clue you talk about," cried the squire, "I will get

PACKET (<u>pak</u> it) *n.*
    a small container
        Synonyms: bundle, parcel

STITCH (<u>stich</u>) *n.*
    a closing made with thread, often used to close
    up a wound
        Synonym: closing loops

ENTRY (<u>en</u> tree) *n.*
    information that is recorded in a book
        Synonyms: note, account

SCOUNDREL (<u>skoun</u> druhl) *n.*
    someone who is evil or disreputable
        Synonyms: villain, rogue

a ship at <u>Bristol</u> dock and take you and Hawkins along with me. We'll have that treasure if I have to search a year."

"Very well," said the doctor. "Now, then, let's open the **packet**!" He placed it on the table.

The bundle was sewn together, and the doctor had to get out his instrument case and cut the **stitches** with his <u>medical</u> scissors. It contained two things, a book and a sealed paper.

The next ten or twelve pages were filled with curious **entries**. There was a date at one end of the line, and at the other end of the line was a sum of money. The record lasted over twenty years, and the amount of the entries grew larger as time went on. At the very end, there was a grand total.

Cried the squire. "This is the black-hearted pirate's <u>account book</u>! These crosses stand for the names of ships or towns that these pirates robbed! The sums are the **scoundrel's** share of the money he stole from them!"

"And now," said the squire, "Let's look at the other paper."

The paper had been sealed in several places.

BULK (bulk) *n.*

the greatest amount of something

Synonyms: most, majority

SKELETON (sk<u>el</u> uh tuhn) *n.*

the framework of bones that support a body

Synonym: bones

The doctor opened the seals with great care, and there fell out the map of an island, with latitude and longitude, names of hills and bays and everything that would be needed to bring a ship to a safe landing upon the island. The island was about nine miles long and five across, and it had two harbors, and a hill in the centre part marked "The Spy Glass." There were three red crosses. Two were on the north part of the island and one was in the southwest. Beside the southwest cross, in small, neat writing, it said: "**Bulk** of treasure here."

Over on the back of the paper, there was the same handwriting and this information: Tall tree, Spy Glass shoulder. Look for North, North North East.

Skeleton Island East Southeast and East.

Ten feet.

The bar silver is in the north. You can find it by the east, ten <u>fathoms</u> south of the black rock with the face on it.

The arms are in the sand-hill, North at the point of north cape, bearing east and a quarter North.

PASSAGE (<u>pass</u> ij) *n.*
a journey over a body of water
Synonyms: voyage, crossing

DESPERATE (<u>des</u> puh rit) *adj.*
hopeless, in a bad situation
Synonyms: distraught, forlorn

The page was signed J.F. "F" for the pirate Flint!

That was all. I didn't understand any of it, but it filled the squire and Dr. Livesey with delight.

"Livesey," said the squire, "Tomorrow I start for Bristol. In ten days, we'll have the best ship, sir, and the best crew in England. Hawkins shall come as <u>cabin boy</u>. You, Livesey, are ship's doctor; I am admiral. We'll take my men Redruth, Joyce, and Hunter. We'll have good winds, a quick **passage** and not the least bit of difficulty in finding the spot, and the money!"

"Squire Trelawney," said the doctor, "I'll go with you. There's only one man I'm afraid of and that's you because you can't hold your tongue. We are not the only men who know of this paper. These fellows who attacked the inn tonight are bold and **desperate**, and there's probably more of them. They are all after that money. None of us must be alone until we get to sea. Jim and I shall stick together. You'll take Joyce and Hunter when you ride to Bristol. Not one of us must breathe a word of what we've found."

ANTICIPATION (an <u>tiss</u> uh pay shun) *n.*
a feeling of excitement about something that
will happen
Synonym: eagerness

ACRE (<u>ay</u> kur) *n.*
an area equal to 43,560 square feet
Synonyms: land, space

MULTITUDE (<u>mulh</u> tuh tood) *n.*
a large number
Synonyms: mass, abundance

"Livesey," said the squire, "You are always right! I'll be as silent as the grave."

It took us a while before we were ready for the sea. I was full of dreams and **anticipations** of strange islands and adventures. I studied the map for hours. In my imagination, I explored every **acre** of its surface. Sometimes the isle was thick with savages, and we fought them. Sometimes it was full of dangerous animals that hunted us.

Finally, we set out for Bristol. The squire had found a ship, the *Hispaniola,* which he had gotten from an old friend named Blandly. The squire was not to tell anyone about our trip, which worried me some. But then again, he not only had a ship, but a crew, as well, lead by someone he called Long John Silver. Silver had lost a leg in his country's service.

Just before we left, I said good-bye to Mother and the cove where I had lived since I was born. I had my first attack of tears. Then I left, and soon my home was out of sight.

We went to Bristol and walked to the ships. To my great delight, I saw a great **multitude** of ships of all sizes from many different countries. In one

STOUT (stowt) *adj.*
strong and thick
Synonyms: bulky, weighty

TAVERN (<u>tav</u> urn) *n.*
a place where people drink or dine in an
informal style
Synonyms: inn, pub

ship sailors were singing at their work. In another ship there were men high over my head, hanging to threads that seemed no thicker than a spider's web. Though I had lived by the shore all my life, it seemed new to me, as if I had never seen it before. The smell of tar and salt was something new. I saw the most wonderful <u>figureheads</u>, that had all been far over the ocean. I saw many old sailors with ear-rings and pigtails, and I could not have been more delighted if these sailors had been kings.

And now I was going to sea myself, bound for an unknown island to seek for buried treasure!

While I was still in this delightful dream, we came suddenly in front of a large inn and met Squire Trelawney, all dressed out like a sea-officer in **stout** blue cloth.

"Here you are," he cried. "The ship's company complete! We sail tomorrow!"

The squire then gave me a note addressed to John Silver, the man who would be the ship's cook on our voyage. The squire told me I should find John Silver easily at a little **tavern** with a large brass telescope for sign. I set off, overjoyed at this

OPPORTUNITY (op ur <u>too</u> nuh tee) *n.*
the ability to do something
Synonym: chance

INTELLIGENT (in <u>tel</u> uh juhnt) *adj.*
the state of being quick to understand and to learn
Synonyms: bright, brilliant

opportunity to see some more of the ships and the sailors, and I soon found the tavern.

It was a bright enough little place. The customers were mostly sailors, and they talked so loudly that I hung at the door, almost afraid to enter.

As I was waiting, a man came out of a side room, and I was sure he must be Long John Silver. His left leg was cut off close by the hip, and under the left shoulder he carried a crutch. He was very tall and strong, and he was **intelligent** and smiling.

Now, to tell you the truth, from the very first mention of Long John in Squire Trelawney's letter, I had been afraid that he might prove to be the very one-legged sailor that I had watched for so long at the old inn. But one look at the man before me was enough. I had seen the captain and Black Dog and the blind man, Pew, and I thought I knew what a buccaneer was like. A pirate was very different than this clean and pleasant Long John Silver. Why, I was sure of it.

I gathered my courage at once, and walked right up to the man.

"Mr. Silver, sir?" I asked, holding out the note.

GRASP (grassp) *n.*
a firm hold
Synonyms: grip, clutch

ATTRACT (uh <u>trakt</u>) *v.* **-ing, -ed**
to be pulled towards something
Synonyms: engage, fascinate

SUSPICION (suh <u>spish</u> uhn) *n.*
a state of uncertainty
Synonyms: doubt, misgiving

"Yes, my lad," said he. And then as he saw the squire's letter.

"Oh!" said he, offering his hand. "I see. You are our new cabin-boy! I'm pleased to see you!" And he took my hand in his **grasp**.

Just then one of the customers at the far side rose suddenly and ran quickly outside. His hurry had **attracted** my notice, and I recognized him at a glance. "Oh," I cried, "stop him! It's Black Dog!"

"I don't care who he is," cried Silver. "He hasn't paid his bill. Harry, run and catch him!"

One of the others who was nearest the door leaped up and ran after him.

"Who did you say he was?" he asked. "Black what?"

"Dog, sir," said I. "Has Mr. Trelawney not told you of the buccaneers? He was one of them."

Silver paused. "Let's see! Black Dog? He used to come here with a blind beggar?"

"The blind beggar's name was Pew!" I cried.

"It was!" cried Silver, now quite excited. "Pew!"

My **suspicions** had grown stronger when I found Black Dog here again. I watched Silver, but

NAUTICAL (<u>naw</u> tuh kuhl) *adj.*
relating to ships or sailing
Synonym: naval

he was too clever for me, and by then the man came back and said that he had lost the track of Black Dog.

Silver and I walked back to the inn where the squire and the doctor were. Along the way, he made himself a most interesting companion, telling me about the different ships that we passed. He told stories about ships and repeated one or another **nautical** phrase until I had learned it perfectly. I began to see that he was the best of shipmates.

When we got to the inn, the squire and Dr. Livesey were seated together, waiting for us before they would go aboard and look at the schooner.

Long John told the story about Black Dog with spirit. "That was how it were, now, weren't it, Hawkins?" he would say, and I always agreed.

The two gentlemen were sorry that Black Dog had got away, but we all agreed there was nothing to be done. Then, Long John left us.

"All hands aboard by four this afternoon," shouted the squire after him.

"Now Jim," says squire. "Take your hat, and we'll see the ship."

SQUINT (skwint) *n.*
a way of looking while holding one's eyes
partly open
Synonyms: glance, stare

OBSERVE (ob serv) *v.* **-ing, -ed**
to watch and study attentively
Synonyms: examine, view

CRUISE (krooz) *n.*
a trip taken on a ship or boat; often it is a long
voyage
Synonyms: voyage, trip

CHAPTER 4

At last, we got on the *Hispaniola*. The mate, Mr. Arrow, an old sailor with earrings and a **squint**, met and saluted us. He and the squire were very friendly, but I soon **observed** that things were not the same between Mr. Trelawney and the captain, Captain Smollett, a sharp-looking man who seemed angry with everything on board.

The captain came over to us. "Squire," said the captain, "I don't like this **cruise**. I don't like the men, and I don't like my officer."

"Why not?" asked Doctor Livesey.

RISK (risk) *n.*

the act of doing something that might be
harmful or dangerous

Synonyms: gamble, chance, hazard

FAMILIAR (fuh <u>mil</u> yur) *adj.*

1. informal

Synonyms: close, friendly

2. well known

Synonyms: common, normal

"I find that every sailor knows more than I do. I don't call that fair. Next, I learn we are going after treasure. I don't like treasure voyages on any account. And I don't like them, above all, when they are secret and when the secret has been blabbed. It seems to me that this trip could be our deaths."

"Well," replied Dr. Livesey. "We take the **risk**. Are the crew not good seamen?"

"I don't like them, sir," said Captain Smollett. "And I think I should have been able to choose my own men."

"Perhaps you should," replied the doctor. "My friend Silver should, perhaps, have taken you along with him when he chose a crew. But we did not think we had done anything wrong. And you don't like Mr. Arrow?"

"I don't, sir. I believe he's a good seaman, but he's too informal with the crew to be a good offi-cer. A mate should keep himself to himself and he shouldn't be too **familiar** with the men."

"Plus," the captain continued. "The gun powder should be kept apart from the arms, for

RESIGN (ruh <u>zine</u>) *v.* **-ing, -ed**
to voluntarily leave a job
Synonyms: quit, give notice

MUTINY (<u>myoo</u> tuh nee) *n.*
a rebellion against someone in charge,
especially on a ship
Synonyms: revolt, uprising

PRECAUTION (pri <u>kaw</u> shuhn) *n.*
an action taken in order to prevent something
unpleasant or dangerous
Synonyms: safeguard, preventative measure

safety reasons. All your crew should be <u>berthed</u> together. And there should be no more blabbing about the treasure. Myself, I've heard that you have a map of an island, that there's crosses on the map to show where treasure is, and where the island lies." And then he named the <u>latitude</u> and <u>longitude</u> exactly.

"I never told any of that," cried the squire. "Not to anyone!"

"The hands know it, sir," said the captain. "I don't know who has this map. But it should be kept secret even from me and Mr. Arrow. Otherwise, I would ask you to let me **resign**."

"I see," said the doctor. "You fear a **mutiny**."

"Sir," said Captain Smollett, "I am responsible for the ship's safety and the life of every man aboard. I see things not going right. And I ask you to take **precautions** or let me resign."

"We will keep an eye out," said the doctor.

"That's as you please, sir," said the captain. "You'll find I do my duty."

And then he left.

"Trelawney," said the doctor, "I believed you

SUPERINTEND (<u>soop</u> ur uhn tend) *v.* **-ing**, **-ed**
to be in charge, to give orders
Synonyms: supervise, oversee

CHORUS (<u>kor</u> ruhz) *n.*
a part of a song that is repeated after each verse
Synonym: refrain

SLUMBER (<u>slum</u> ber) *n.*
sleep
Synonyms: snooze, shuteye

have two honest men on board with you, that man and John Silver."

"Silver is honest," cried the squire, "but I'm not so sure about this man."

"Well," says the doctor, "we'll see."

When we came on deck, the men had begun already to take out the arms and gunpowder, yo-ho-ing at their work, while the captain and Mr. Arrow stood by **superintending**.

We were all hard at work, putting the powder away from the arms, changing the berths, when the last man or two, and Long John along with them, came abroad in a boat.

All that night we were putting things in their places. Long John Silver began to sing, "Fifteen men on the dead man's chest—"

And then the whole crew sang the **chorus**:

"Yo-ho-ho, and a bottle of rum!"

Soon the anchor was pulled up, and the sails were put up, too. Before I could grab an hour of **slumber**, the *Hispaniola* had begun her voyage to the Treasure Island!

I am not going to tell about the voyage in

DETAIL (<u>dee</u> tayl) *n.*
the small or minor parts of something
Synonyms: specific, particular

CAPABLE (<u>kape</u> uh buhl) *adj.*
able to do something well
Synonyms: qualified, competent

detail. The ship proved to be a good ship, the crew were **capable** seamen, and the captain understood his business. But before we came to Treasure Island, two or three things happened which I must tell.

Mr. Arrow, first of all, turned out even worse than the captain had feared. He had no command among the men, and people did what they pleased with him. He got drunker and drunker, though no one knew where he got the drink, and one day he simply fell <u>overboard</u> and was not seen again.

There we were, though without a mate, and it was necessary, of course, to make one of the men our mate. The <u>boatswain</u>, Job Anderson, was the likeliest man aboard, and he became our mate. And the <u>coxswain</u>, Israel Hands, was a careful, old, experienced seaman who could be trusted with almost anything. He was also a great friend of our cook, Long John Silver, whom he called <u>Barbecue</u>.

All the crew respected and even obeyed Silver. He had a way of talking to each and doing everybody some service. To me he was kind, and he was always glad to see me in the <u>galley</u>, which

PREDICT (pruh <u>dikt</u>) *v.* **-ing, -ed**
to say what might happen in the future
Synonyms: speculate, foresee

BRISK (brisk) *adj.*
quick and lively
Synonyms: active, spry

he kept as clean as a new pin, the dishes hanging up and his parrot in a cage in one corner.

"Come away, Hawkins," he would say, "come and sit and tell yarns with me. Nobody more welcome than yourself, son. Sit you down and hear the news. Here's Cap'n Flint – I calls my parrot Cap'n Flint, after the famous buccaneer – **predicting** success to our voyage. Wasn't you, Cap'n?"

And the parrot would scream out, "Pieces of eight! Pieces of eight! Pieces of eight!"

In the meantime, the squire and Captain Smollett were still pretty unhappy with one another. The squire hated the captain. The captain, on his part, never spoke but when he was spoken to and then sharp and short and dry. Not a word wasted. He finally said that he seemed to have been wrong about the crew, that some of them were as **brisk** as he wanted to see and all had behaved well. As for the ship, he had taken a liking to her. The squire, though, still did not like him.

It was about the last day of our voyage. We

OCCUR (uh <u>kur</u>) *v.* **-ing, -ed**
   1. to have an idea come to mind
      Synonym: spring to mind
   2. to take place
      Synonyms: happen, transpire

GENTLY (<u>jent</u> lee) *adv.*
   to do something very softly or lightly
      Synonyms: mildly, tenderly

were to reach the Treasure Island some time that night, or by noon. The *Hispaniola* rolled steadily. Everyone was in the bravest spirits because we were now so near an end of our adventure.

Now, just after sundown, when all my work was over and I was on my way to my berth, it **occurred** to me that I should like an apple from the apple barrel down below. I ran on deck. The watch was looking out to sea for the island. Another sailor was watching the sail and whistling away **gently** to himself, and that was the only sound except the swish of the sea around the sides of the ship.

I climbed inside the apple barrel, and found there was not an apple left. I sat down and the waters and rocking movement of the ship put me at the point of falling asleep when a heavy man sat down close by me. The barrel shook as he leaned his shoulders against it, and I was just about to jump up when the man began to speak. It was Silver's voice, and before I had heard a dozen words I would not have shown myself for all the world. I lay there, trembling and listening, in fear and curiosity, for from these dozen words I understood that the

ADMIRATION (ad muh <u>ray</u> shun) *n.*
a feeling of approval and liking
Synonyms: regard, esteem

FLATTERY (<u>flat</u> uh ree) *n.*
praise that is not sincere
Synonyms: sweet talk, puffery

lives of all the honest men aboard depended upon me alone.

"No, not I," said Silver. "Flint was the captain. Flint's ship was filled with gold."

"Ah!" cried another voice, that of the youngest hand on board, and full of **admiration**. "He was a smart and great man, was that pirate Flint!"

"I had nine hundred pounds from England and two thousand from Flint," said Silver. "And where's all England's men now? I don't know. Where's Flint's? Why, most on 'em aboard here, and glad of it. You're young, you are, but you're as smart as paint. I'll talk to you like a man about how to keep the treasure you find and how to keep yourself alive."

You may imagine how I felt when I heard this old rogue addressing another in the very same words of **flattery** that he had used to myself. I think, if I had been able, that I would have killed him through the barrel. Meantime, he ran on, little knowing he was overheard.

"Here it is about pirates. They lives rough, and they risk being hanged, and when a cruise is

FLING (fling) *n.*
a brief period of enjoyment
Synonyms: party, good time, spree

DAINTY (<u>dane</u> tee) *adj.*
delicate, small, and delicious
Synonyms: pleasing, lovely

done, why, they have hundreds of <u>pounds</u> instead of hundreds of <u>farthings</u> in their pockets.

"Now," he went on, "the most goes for rum and a good **fling**, and then they have to go to sea again. But that's not the course I lay. I puts my money all away, some here, some there, and none too much anywheres, so no one gets suspicious. I'm fifty years old. And once back from this cruise, I plan to set myself up as a gentlemen. It's about time, too. Ah, but I've lived easy in the meantime, never stopped myself from having anything I wanted. I've slept on soft beds and ate **dainty** food, except at sea. And how did I begin? I was a sailor, like you!"

Silver sighed. "My Spy-Glass Inn is sold. My old missis has most of my money now, and I'll meet up with her sometime to get it."

"Well, I tell you now," said the lad, "I didn't really like this job till I had this talk with you, John. But now I shall join with you and be a pirate."

"And a brave lad you were and smart too," answered Silver, shaking hands so heartily that all the barrel shook.

CORRUPTION (kor <u>up</u> shun) *n.*
the action of making someone become
dishonest or immoral
Synonyms: decay, infection, demoralization

STROLL (strol) *v.* **-ing**, **-ed**
to take a leisurely walk
Synonyms: ramble, saunter, promenade

SOBER (<u>sobe</u> ur) *adj.*
not being under the influence of alcohol
or drugs
Synonyms: not drunk, level-headed

By this time I had begun to understand that the little scene that I had overheard was the last act in the **corruption** of one of the honest hands, perhaps of the last one left aboard. Silver gave a little whistle, a third man **strolled** up and sat down by the party.

"Dick's with us," said Silver.

"Oh, I know'd Dick was," returned the voice of the coxswain, Israel Hands. "But when are we going to act? I've had almost enough of Cap'n Smollett. He's bossed me around long enough, by thunder! I want to go into that cabin, I do. I want their pickles and wines. I want a mutiny."

"Israel," said Silver, "You'll speak softly, and you'll keep **sober** till I give the word."

"Well, I don't say no, do I?" growled the coxswain. "What I say is, when? That's what I say."

"When!" cried Silver. "Well, I'll tell you when. When it's the right time, and that's when. Here's a first-rate seaman, Cap'n Smollett, who knows how to sail the ship for us. Here's this squire and doctor with a treasure map that we need to find the treasure. I don't know where it is, do I? No more

NAVIGATE (<u>nav</u> uh gayt) *v.* **-ing**, **-ed**
to plan and control travel using maps, charts, or stars
Synonyms: direct, guide

MAROONED (mah <u>roond</u>) *adj.*
abandoned without a way to escape
Synonyms: shipwrecked, stranded

than you do. Well then, I mean this squire and doctor shall find the treasure for us, and help us to get it aboard. Then we'll see. Why, I'd have Cap'n Smollett **navigate** us half-way back again before I struck. I'll finish with them at the island, as soon's the treasure's on board, and a pity it is," said Silver.

"But," asked Dick, "what are we to do with 'em, anyhow?"

"Well, what would you think?" cried the cook. "Put 'em ashore and have them be **marooned**? Or cut 'em down like that much pork? That would have been Flint's, or Billy Bones's, way to do it."

"Billy was the man for that," said Israel. "Well, he's dead now."

"Right you are," said Silver; "I give my vote. Death. We kill them all. When I'm back in England and have lots of money, I don't want anyone coming to look for me and asking me where I got it. We will wait to kill them, though, is what I say. But when the time comes, we do it fast. But I claim Trelawney. I'll wring his head off his body with these hands, Dick!" he added, breaking off.

LIMB (limb) *n.*
an arm or leg
Synonyms: appendage, member

ABSENCE (<u>ab</u> suhnse) *n.*
the state of not being present
Synonyms: elsewhere, nonattendance

AUDIBLE (<u>aw</u> duh buhl) *adj.*
loud enough to be heard
Synonyms: hearable, detectable

"I'm hungry now, I am. You just jump up, like a sweet lad, and get me an apple."

What terror I was in! I should have leaped out and run for it if I had found the strength, but my **limbs** were weak as water. I heard Dick begin to rise, and then someone seemingly stopped him, and a voice shouted, "Oh, stop that! Let's have some rum!"

"Dick," said Silver, "There's the key. You go bring it up."

Terrified as I was, I could not help thinking to myself that this must have been how Mr. Arrow got the rum that destroyed him.

Dick was gone but a little while, and during his **absence** Israel spoke quietly to Silver in a voice that was barely **audible**. "Not another man of them'll join us," he said. I took this to mean that there were still faithful men on board.

Just then a sort of brightness fell upon me in the barrel, and, looking up, I found the moon had risen and was shining white. Almost at the same time the voice of the lookout shouted, "Land ho!"

CONGREGATED (<u>kong</u> gruh gayt) *adj.*
gathered together in a group
Synonyms: assembled, convened

HORRID (<u>hor</u> ud) *adj.*
very disagreeable, terrible
Synonyms: gross, hideous

ISSUE (<u>ish</u> oo) *v.* **-ing, -ed**
to send or give out
Synonyms: distribute, dispense

CHAPTER 5

There was a great rush of feet across the deck. I could hear people tumbling up from the cabin. I slipped from my barrel and came out upon the open deck.

There all hands had already **congregated**. I saw everything almost in a dream, because I had not yet gotten over my **horrid** fear of a minute or two before. And then I heard the voice of Captain Smollett **issuing** orders. The *Hispaniola* was now sailing a course that would just clear the island on the east.

CHART (chart) *n.*
  a graph or map giving information
    Synonyms: diagram, blueprint

ANNOYANCE (uh <u>noy</u> uhnce) *n.*
  the feeling or state of being bothered
    Synonyms: irritation, anger, displeasure

"There it is," said Silver. "Skeleton Island they calls it. It were a main place for pirates once, and a hand we had on board knowed all their names for it. That hill they calls the Fore-Mast Hill. There are three hills in a row running south. But the main hill, that's the bit one with a cloud on it, they usually calls it the Spy-Glass, because there is a lookout they kept when their ship was anchored there."

"I have a **chart** here," says Captain Smollett. "See if that's the place."

Long John's eyes burned in his head as he took the chart. By the fresh look of the paper I knew this was not the map we found in the old captain's chest. It was a copy, complete with names and heights and soundings, but there were no red crosses and no written notes. Silver's **annoyance** must have been sharp, but he hid it.

"Yes, sir," said he, "this is the spot, to be sure."

"Thank you, my man," says Captain Smollett, turning to the squire. "I'll ask you later on to give us some help."

I was surprised by how freely John showed his

HORROR (hor ruh) *n.*
   an extreme feeling of fear
      Synonyms: terror, panic

CRUELTY (<u>kroo</u> uhl tee) *n.*
   behavior that causes pain or suffering
      Synonyms: viciousness, brutality,
      heartlessness

CONCEAL (kon <u>seel</u>) *v.* **-ing**, **-ed**
   to place something where it cannot be seen
      Synonyms: hide, cover

SHUDDER (<u>shuhd</u> ur) *n.*
   a shake, usually caused by fear
      Synonyms: tremble, quiver

PRETENCE (<u>pree</u> tense) *n.*
   an untrue action that is meant to deceive
      Synonyms: falsehood, fabrication

knowledge of the island, and I was really frightened when I saw him drawing nearer to myself.
He did not know that I had overheard him from
the apple barrel, and yet I had by this time taken
such a **horror** of his **cruelty** and power that I
could not **conceal** a **shudder** when he laid his
hand upon my arm.

"Ah," says he, "this here is a sweet spot for a
lad to get ashore on. You'll swim, and you'll climb
trees, and you'll hunt goats. When you want to go
a bit of exploring, you just ask old John, and he'll
put up a snack for you to take along."

And clapping me in the friendliest way upon
the shoulder, he walked off.

Captain Smollett, the squire, and Dr. Livesey
were talking together on the <u>quarterdeck</u>. "Doctor,
let me speak to you in secret," I whispered. "Get
the captain and squire down to the cabin, and
then make some **pretence** to send for me. I have
terrible news."

The doctor looked surprised. "Thank you,
Jim, that was all I wanted to know," he said loudly,
as if he had asked me a question.

PLOT (plot) *v.* **-ing**, **-ed**
to come up with a plan
Synonyms: contrive, arrange, scheme

CONVERSATION (kon ver <u>say</u> shun) *n.*
an exchange of ideas in which people speak together
Synonyms: chat, conference

AWAIT (uh <u>wayte</u>) *v.* **-ing**, **-ed**
to wait for something or someone
Synonyms: anticipate, look for

And with that he turned on his heel and joined the other two. The next thing that I heard was the captain giving an order to Job Anderson, and all hands were called on deck.

"My lads," said Captain Smollett, "This land that we have sighted is the place we have been sailing for. Mr. Trelawney and I and the doctor are going below to the cabin to drink *your* health and luck, and you'll have <u>grog</u> served out for you to drink *our* health and luck. And if you think as I do, you'll give a good sea cheer."

The cheer followed, but it rang out so full and hearty that I could hardly believe these same men were **plotting** for our blood.

The three gentlemen went below, and not long after, word was sent that I was wanted in the cabin.

I found them all three seated round the table. "Now, Hawkins," said the squire, "you have something to say. Speak up."

I told them about Silver's **conversation**.

"Now, captain," said the squire, "you were right, and I was wrong. I **await** your orders."

PROPOSE (pruh <u>poze</u>) *v.* **-ing**, **-ed**
to put forward a plan or idea
Synonyms: suggest, offer, submit

"I never heard of a crew that meant to mutiny that didn't first show signs of it coming," said the captain. "First point. We must sail on, because we can't turn back. If I gave the word to turn around, the men would rise against me at once. Second point, we have some time to think what to do, at least until this treasure's found. Third point, there are still some faithful hands. Now, sir, it's got to come to blows sooner or later, and what I **propose** is to come to blows some fine day when they least expect it. There are seven of us I can think of that we can count on. Now, who are all the honest hands?"

"Most likely the ones that Squire Trelawney picked himself, before he picked Silver." said the doctor.

"Well, then," said the captain, "We must keep a lookout for men on our side."

"Jim here," said the doctor, "can help us more than anyone. The men are not shy with him, and Jim notices things."

I began to feel pretty desperate at this, for I felt helpless. In the meantime, talk as we pleased, there were only seven out of the twenty-six men that

SPIRE (spire) *n.*
> a structure that comes to a point on top
>> Synonyms: peak, point

SURF (surf) *n.*
> waves as they break on the shore
>> Synonyms: spray, splash

we knew we could count on. But out of these seven, one was a boy. That meant that the grown men on our side were only six to their nineteen.

I couldn't sleep that night, but when I came on deck the next morning, I saw that the island was changed!

The island was grey, with wild stone **spires**, and foaming noisy **surf** on the beach. The sun shone bright and hot, and the shore birds were fishing and crying all around us. You would have thought anyone would have been glad to get to land after being so long at sea, but I knew what trouble was coming. My heart sank, and I hated the very thought of Treasure Island.

The plunge of our anchor sent up clouds of birds wheeling and crying over the woods, but soon they settled down again. The island was buried in woods, the trees coming right down to the high-water mark, the shores mostly flat, and the hilltops standing round at a distance in a sort of amphitheatre, one here, one there. Two little rivers, or rather two swamps, emptied out into this pond. From the ship we could see nothing of the

CONDUCT (<u>kon</u> duct) *n.*
the way someone behaves
Synonyms: manner, demeanor

ADVICE (ad <u>viz</u>) *n.*
a suggestion given to help make a decision
Synonyms: counsel, recommendation

ANXIETY (ang <u>zye</u> uh tee) *n.*
a feeling of uneasiness or a feeling that
something bad may happen
Synonyms: worry, distress, panic

COUNCIL (<u>kown</u> suhl) *n.*
a meeting of a group of concerned people
Synonyms: conference, gathering

house and stockade that were supposed to be on the island. They were quite buried among trees.

If the **conduct** of the men had been alarming before, it became truly threatening now. They lay about the deck growling together in talk. Any order was received with a black look and was carelessly obeyed. Mutiny, it was plain, now hung over us like a thunder-cloud.

And it was not only we of the cabin party who saw the danger. Long John was hard at work going from group to group, giving out good **advice**. He smiled at everyone. If an order were given, John would be on his crutch in an instant, with the cheeriest "Aye, aye, sir!" in the world. When there was nothing else to do, he kept up one song after another, as if to hide the unhappiness of the rest.

Of all the gloomy doings of that gloomy afternoon, Long John Silver's **anxiety** seemed the worst.

We held a **council** in the cabin.

"Sir," said the captain, "if I risk another order, the whole ship'll mutiny. Now, we've only one man to rely on."

MILD (myld) *adj.*
well-behaved, not excited or violent
Synonyms: gentle, mellow

CONFIDENCE (<u>kon</u> fuh dens) *n.*
the feeling that one can rely on someone or something
Synonym: trust

"And who is that?" asked the squire.

"Silver, sir," returned the captain, "He's as anxious as you and I not to have trouble now. Not before he gets to the treasure! He'd talk them out of trouble now if he had the chance, so let's give him that chance. Let's allow the men an afternoon ashore. If they all go to Silver's side, why, we'll fight them. If they none of them go, well then, we have enough men to keep control of the boat. If some go to Silver, he'll still want them to keep calm until it's time to strike. So he'll bring 'em aboard again as **mild** as lambs and then we can figure out how to deal with them."

It was so decided. Loaded pistols were served out to all the men that we were sure were on our side. Hunter, Joyce, and Redruth were taken into our **confidence** and received the news with less surprise and a better spirit than we had looked for. Then the captain went on deck and talked to the crew.

"My lads," said he, "we've had a hot day and are tired. Time on shore will hurt nobody. The boats are still in the water. You can take the

IDLE (<u>eye</u> duhl) *adj.*
not doing anything
Synonyms: lazy, slothful

SULK (sulk) *v.* **-ing, -ed**
to be withdrawn or sullen
Synonyms: pout, mope

INNOCENT (<u>in</u> uh sent) *adj.*
not guilty; having goodness
Synonyms: pure, blameless

gigs, and go ashore for the afternoon. I'll fire a gun half an hour before sundown to let you know when it's time to come back."

I believe the pirates must have thought they would find treasure as soon as they were landed, for they all gave a cheer.

The captain went out of sight in a moment, leaving Silver to arrange the party, and I thought it was as well he did so. Had he been on deck, he could no longer have pretended not to know what was really going on. It was as plain as day. Silver was the captain, and his crew was ready for a fight.

Why did some of the honest hands go with Silver? I knew a few were good fellows for the most part, but the trip here was a hard one. These sailors could not be led nor driven any further. They needed some time off. I told myself there was no danger. It is one thing for a sailor to be **idle** and **sulk** and quite another to take a ship and murder a number of **innocent** men.

At last, however, the party was made up. Six fellows were to stay on board, and the remaining thirteen, plus Silver, began to leave.

REGRET (ruh <u>gret</u>) *v.* **-ing, -ed**
  to feel sorry about having done something
    Synonyms: lament, feel remorse

HEED (heed) *n.*
  careful attention
    Synonyms: concern, consideration

I began to have an idea. If the thirteen men who had left the ship came back and tried to take the ship from us, the six men left on board could not beat them. If the thirteen men did not come back for trouble, then the six men left on ship were more than enough to take care of business. They had no need of me! I should go ashore at once! I slipped over the side of the boat and curled up in the nearest boat, and almost at the same moment, the boat began to sail towards shore.

No one took notice of me. But Silver, from the other boat, looked sharply over and called out to know if that were me, and from that moment I began to **regret** what I had done.

The crews raced for the beach, and my boat got there first. I ran onto the island, while Silver and the rest were still a hundred yards behind.

"Jim, Jim!" I heard him shouting.

But you may suppose I paid no **heed**. Jumping, I ran straight until I could run no longer.

I was so pleased at having given the slip to Long John that I began to enjoy myself and look around me at the strange land that I was in.

EXPLORATION (ek spluh <u>ray</u> shuhn) *n.*
the search and study of something
Synonyms: discovery, investigation

UNINHABITED (un in <u>hab</u> uh tid) *adj.*
without people
Synonyms: desolate, barren

HISS (hiss) *v.* **-ing, -ed**
to make an "sss" noise
Synonym: buzz

CHAPTER 6

I was on an open piece of sandy country, about a mile long, dotted with a great number of trees. I now felt for the first time the joy of **exploration**. The isle was **uninhabited**, my shipmates I had left behind, and nothing lived in front of me but animals. I ran among the trees. Here and there were flowering plants, unknown to me. Here and there I saw snakes, and one raised his head from a rock and **hissed** at me.

Soon I heard the very distant and low tones of a <u>human</u> voice, which, grew louder and nearer.

OBVIOUS (<u>ob</u> vee uhs) *adj.*
    easy to see or understand
        Synonyms: clear, apparent

DRAW (draw) *v.* **-ing, -ed**
    to pull or move something (or someone) in a
    specific direction
        Synonyms: move, gather

This put me in a great fear, and I crawled under cover of the nearest oak and hid there, silent as a mouse.

Another voice answered, and then the first voice, which I now recognized to be Silver's. Since I had been so foolish as to come ashore with these pirates, the least I could do was to overhear them at their councils. My plain and **obvious** duty, therefore, was to **draw** as close as I could to them.

Crawling on all fours, I moved slowly towards them, till at last, raising my head to an opening among the leaves, I could see where Long John Silver and another of the crew stood face to face in conversation.

"Mate," Silver was saying, "I'm warning you. You can't change the plan. The only way you can save your neck is to join with us. And if one of the wild ones knew I was telling you any of this, what do you think would happen to me?"

"Silver," 'said the other man and I saw it was a sailor named Tom, "I'd sooner lose my hand than join with you. If I turn against my duty—"

DEFY (duh <u>fye</u>) *v.* **-ing, -ed**
To refuse to submit
Synonyms: disobey, challenge

MISSILE (<u>miss</u> uhl) *n.*
a weapon that is thrown or shot at a target
Synonyms: bullet, rocket, dart

And then all of a sudden he was interrupted by a noise. A death yell. "In heaven's name, tell me, what was that?" Tom cried.

"That?" returned Silver, smiling away at him. "That? Oh, I think that scream came from Alan."

"Alan!" Tom cried. "You've killed Alan? You're a mate of mine no more, Silver. If I die like a dog, I'll die in my duty. Kill me too, if you can. But I **defy** you."

And with that, this brave fellow turned his back directly on the cook and set off walking for the beach. But he was not to go far. With a cry John seized the branch of a tree, whipped the crutch out of his armpit, and sent it like a **missile** through the air. It struck poor Tom, right between the shoulders in the middle of his back. His hands flew up, he gave a sort of gasp and fell.

Silver was on the top of him next moment and twice buried his knife in Tom's body.

The whole world swam away from before me in a mist. Silver and the birds and the tall Spy-Glass hilltop were going round and round before my eyes.

MONSTER (<u>mohn</u> ster) *n.*
a creature with a scary appearance
Synonyms: beast, freak

THICKET (<u>thik</u> it) *n.*
a dense growth of bushes
Synonyms: grove, copse

FIEND (feend) *n.*
an evil or horrible person
Synonyms: devil, demon

There were all manner of bells ringing and distant voices shouting in my ear. I fainted.

When I came out of my faint, the **monster** had pulled himself together, his crutch under his arm, his hat upon his head. But now John put his hand into his pocket, brought out a whistle, and blew upon it several blasts that rang far across the heated air. I could not tell, of course, the meaning of the signal, but it instantly awoke my fears. More men would be coming. I might be discovered. They had already killed two of the honest people, Tom and Alan. Would I be next?

Instantly I began to crawl back again, with what speed and silence I could manage, to the more open part of the wood. As I did so, I could hear cries coming and going between the old buccaneer and his comrades, and this sound of danger lent me wings. As soon as I was clear of the **thicket**, I ran as I never ran before, and as I ran, fear grew and grew upon me.

Could anyone be more lost than I? When the gun fired, how should I dare to go down to the boats among those **fiends**? Would not the first

EVIDENCE (<u>eh</u> vuh dens) *n.*
>one or more reasons to think that something is true or false
>>Synonyms: proof, documentation

NOTICE (noh tiss) *n.*
>an advance announcement
>>Synonyms: warning, clue

of them who saw me kill me? And if they didn't see me, wouldn't they take that as **evidence** that I knew what they had done and was too scared to show myself? It was all over, I thought. Good-bye to the *Hispaniola*! Good-bye to the squire, the doctor, and the captain! There was nothing left for me but death by the hands of the pirates.

All this while, as I say, I was still running, and without taking any **notice**, I had drawn near to the foot of the little hill and had got into a part of the island where the oaks grew.

And here a fresh alarm brought me to a stop with a thumping heart.

From the side of the hill, I saw a figure leap behind the trunk of a pine.

I was now, it seemed, cut off upon both sides. Behind me were the murderers, before me, this thing. And then, suddenly, Silver himself appeared, less terrible than this creature of the woods, and I turned and ran towards the boats.

Instantly the figure reappeared, and began to head me off. I was about to call for help, but I told myself he was a man, however wild. That

REASSURE (<u>re</u> uh shur) *v.* **-ing, -ed**
to help someone feel less worried
Synonyms: comfort, guarantee

REVIVE (ruh <u>vyve</u>) *v.* **-ing, -ed**
to return to life
Synonyms: bring to, start again, awake

HESITATE (<u>hez</u> uh tate) *v.*
to stop for a time before doing something
Synonyms: pause, wait

somewhat **reassured** me, even as my fear of Silver began to **revive**.

I remembered my pistol. Courage grew again in my heart, and I walked towards this strange man of the island.

He was hidden by this time behind another tree trunk. But he must have been watching me closely, for as soon as I began to move to him, he appeared and took a step to meet me. Then he **hesitated**, drew back, came forward again, and at last, to my wonder, threw himself on his knee and held out his hands to me.

"Who are you?" I asked.

"Ben Gunn," he answered, and his voice sounded awkward, as if he had not used it in a long time. "I'm poor Ben Gunn, I am, and I haven't spoken with a man these three years."

I could now see that he was a man like myself. His skin was burnt by the sun. His clothes were all torn.

"Three years!" I cried. "Were you ship-wrecked?"

"Nay, mate," said he, "I was marooned."

PUNISHMENT (pun ish ment) *n.*
an action taken because someone has done
something wrong
Synonyms: correction, penalty

OFFENDER (uh <u>fen</u> der) *n.*
one who commits a crime
Synonyms: criminal, lawbreaker

SOLITUDE (<u>sol</u> uh tood) *n.*
the state of being without people
Synonyms: loneliness, seclusion

I had heard the word, and I knew it stood for a horrible kind of **punishment** common enough among the buccaneers, in which the **offender** is put ashore with little supplies and left behind on some island.

"Marooned three years ago," he said, "and I lived on goats since then, and berries and oysters. You don't have any cheese on you, do you?"

"If ever I can get aboard again," said I, "you shall have cheese."

"If ever you can get aboard again, says you?" he repeated. "Why, now, who's to stop you?"

"Not you, I know," I said.

"No, I wouldn't stop you," he cried. "Now what do you call yourself, mate?"

"Jim," I told him.

"Jim, Jim," says he, quite pleased. "Well, now, Jim, I've lived so rough, you'd be ashamed to hear of it. But, Jim" he whispered. He looked all around himself and then lowered his voice even more. "I'm rich!" he said.

I now felt sure that the poor fellow had gone crazy in his **solitude**, and I must have shown the

ALLY (<u>al</u> lye) *n.*

someone who provides help or assistance

Synonyms: partner, associate

WRING (ring) *n.*

a painful turn

Synonyms: twist, wrench

PREDICAMENT (pruh <u>dik</u> a ment) *n.*

a bad situation that is hard to get out of

Synonyms: trouble, mess

KEENEST (<u>keen</u> est) *adj.*

most eager

Synonyms: intense, zealous

feeling in my face, for he grew angry. "Rich! Rich! I am rich!" he said. "And you'll bless your stars, you will, that you found me!"

And at this there came suddenly a shadow over his face.

"Now, Jim, you tell me true. That ain't Flint's ship over there?" he asked.

At this I began to believe that I had found an **ally**, and I answered him at once.

"It's not Flint's ship, and Flint is dead. But there are some of Flint's hands aboard."

"Not a man with one leg?" he gasped.

"Silver?" I asked.

"Ah, Silver!" says he. "I know of Silver!"

"He's the cook and the leader too."

He was still holding me by the wrist, and at that he give it quite a **wring**.

"If you was sent by Long John," he said, "I'm as good as dead, and I know it."

I told him the whole story of our voyage and the **predicament** in which we found ourselves. He heard me with the **keenest** interest, and when I had done he patted me on the head.

VESSEL (<u>vess</u> uhl) *n.*
a craft for traveling on water
Synonyms: boat, ship

"You're a good lad, Jim," he said; "Well, you just put your trust in Ben Gunn. Would you think it likely, now, that your squire would help me?"

I told him the squire most surely would.

"Aye, but you see," returned Ben Gunn, "I didn't mean helping me by just giving me clothes and such. I told you there's money here. Would he share it and not take it all for his own? Would he give to me one thousand pounds?"

"I am sure he would," said I.

"*And* a passage home?" he added.

"Why," I cried, "the squire's a gentleman. And besides, if we got rid of the others, we should want you to help work the **vessel** home."

"Ah," said he, relieved. "so you would."

"Now, I'll tell you what," he went on. "I was in Flint's ship when he buried the treasure with six other strong seamen. They all went ashore for a week. One fine day, up went the signal, and here come Flint by himself in a little boat and the six all dead and buried. How he done it, not a man aboard us could make out. It was battle, murder, and sudden death, him against six. Billy Bones was the

119

SPADE (spayd) *n.*
a tool used for digging
Synonym: shovel, trowel

mate. Long John, he was <u>quartermaster</u>. And they asked Flint where the treasure was. 'Ah,' says he, 'You can go ashore, if you like, and stay,' he says; 'but as for the ship, she's leaving!'

"Well, I was in another ship three years back, and we sighted this island. 'Boys,' said I, 'here's Flint's treasure; let's land and find it.'

"The cap'n was not happy about that," he went on. "But we all went to find the treasure anyway. We looked for it for twelve days, and every day the crew got madder and madder at me until one fine morning all hands went aboard. 'As for you, Benjamin Gunn,' says they, 'here's a <u>musket</u>,' they says, 'and a **spade** and a pick-axe. You can stay here and find Flint's money for yourself.'

"Well, Jim, three years have I been here, and I have not had a bite of good food. But I have changed. You tell your squire that Gunn is a good man now and not a pirate. You tell him that Gunn is one to be trusted."

"Well," I said, "I don't understand one word that you've been saying. But how am I to get on board?"

INTERVAL (<u>in</u> ter vuhl) *n.*

the time between two events
Synonyms: break, period

VOLLEY (<u>vol</u> lee) *n.*

a burst of shots, the firing of bullets at the same
time
Synonyms: attack, outbreak

ARM (arm) *n.*

firearm, a weapon using gun powder and
bullets
Synonym: gun

"Ah," said he, "Well, there's my boat, that I made with my two hands. I keep her under the white rock. If the worst come to the worst, we might try that after dark. Hi!" he broke out. "What's that?"

For just then, we heard thunder of a cannon.

"They have begun to fight!" I cried. "Follow me."

And I began to run towards the ship, while close at my side the marooned man trotted easily.

"Left, left," says he; "keep to your left, Jim! Under the trees with you!"

The cannon-shot was followed after a considerable **interval** by a **volley** of small **arms**.

Another pause, and then, not a quarter of a mile in front of me, I saw the Union Jack flag flutter in the air above a wood.

WANTING (<u>wahnt</u> ing) *adj.*
not being sufficient or enough
Synonyms: lacking, inadequate

CHAPTER 7

The Tale Is Taken Up by Doctor Livesey

It was about half past one that the two boats went ashore from the *Hispaniola*. The captain, the squire, and I were talking matters over in the cabin. Had there been a breath of wind, we should have fallen on the six mutineers who were left aboard with us, and sailed away to sea. But the wind was **wanting**, and to complete our helplessness, Hunter came to tell us the news that Jim Hawkins had gone ashore with the rest.

QUEST (kwest) *n.*
a journey to look for something
Synonyms: search, hunt

We never thought to doubt Jim Hawkins, but we were alarmed for his safety. We ran on deck. The six scoundrels were sitting grumbling under a sail. Ashore we could see the gigs made fast and a man sitting in each. Waiting was hard, and it was decided that Hunter and I should go ashore in **quest** of information.

Hunter and I went in the direction of the stockade upon the chart. The two who were left guarding their boats seemed to be discussing what they ought to do. Had they gone and told Silver, all might have turned out differently, but they had their orders, I suppose, and decided to sit quietly.

We landed, and I jumped out and came running with pistols ready.

I had not gone a hundred yards when I reached the stockade. There was a house built of logs there, fit to hold twenty people. It had a good strong door, and it was <u>loopholed</u> for guns on either side. Short of a complete surprise, the people inside might have held the place against a <u>regiment</u>.

They also had a spring. On the boat, we had plenty of arms and things to eat, but there had

ACCOMPLISHMENT (uh <u>kom</u> plish ments) *n.*
something that has been done, especially
something done well
Synonyms: success, triumph

HAIL (hale) *v.* **-ing, -ed**
to shout to get someone's attention
Synonyms: call, flag down

been no water. Suddenly, there came ringing over the island the cry of a man at the point of death. "Jim Hawkins is gone," was my first thought.

I made up my mind and returned to the shore and jumped on board the little boat we came in. Hunter and I made the water fly, and we were soon aboard the schooner.

I found the men all shaken, as was natural. The squire was sitting down, as white as a sheet, thinking of the harm he had led us to, the good man!

I told my plan to the captain, and between us we settled on the details of its **accomplishment**.

We put one man, old Redruth, in the gallery with three or four loaded muskets for protection. Hunter brought the boat round, and Joyce and I set to work loading her with powder tins, muskets, bags of <u>biscuits</u>, pork, and my medicine chest.

In the meantime, the squire and the captain stayed on deck. The captain **hailed** the coxswain, who was the main man aboard.

"Mr. Hands," he said, "there are two of us here, and we each have pistols. If any one of you six make a signal, that man's dead."

CONSULTATION (kon sul <u>tay</u> shun) *n.*
a meeting held to talk about something
Synonyms: conference, discussion

PROVISIONS (pro <u>vih</u> shun) *n.*
necessary items such as food, a weapon, or
clothing that one has on hand
Synonyms: supplies, stocks

CARGO (<u>kar</u> goh) *n.*
freight carried by a ship
Synonyms: baggage, goods, shipment

They were a good deal taken aback, and after a little **consultation** one and all tumbled below deck, to find Redruth waiting for them. They came up again, and they sat very still.

We had the little boat loaded as much as we dared. Leaving the captain, the squire, and old Redruth to hold the mutineers, Hunter, Joyce and I made for shore as fast as oars could take us.

We had soon touched land in the same place as before and set to bring **provisions** to the block house. Then, leaving Joyce to guard them, Hunter and I returned to the boat and loaded ourselves once more. So we kept going without pausing to take a breath, till the whole **cargo** was unloaded to the block house.

That we should have risked a second boatload seems more daring than it really was. None of the men ashore had a musket, as we did, and before they could get within range for pistol shooting, we thought we could kill a half-dozen at least.

When we arrived back at the *Hispaniola,* the squire was waiting for me at the window. We fell to loading the boat for our very lives. The rest of

RESUME (ruh <u>zoom</u>) *v.* **-ing, -ed**
to begin again
Synonyms: restart, proceed

SCUFFLE (<u>skuf</u> fuhl) *n.*
a struggle
Synonyms: fight, commotion, brawl

the arms and powder we dropped overboard. Redruth left his place in the gallery and dropped into the boat.

"Now, men," called Captain Smollet to the men below deck, "Do you hear me?"

There was no answer.

"Abraham Gray! I'm speaking to you!" the captain shouted.

Still no reply.

"Gray," **resumed** Mr. Smollett, a little louder, "I am leaving this ship, and I order you to follow your captain. I know you are a good man. I give you thirty seconds to leave these pirates who are with you and come and join me."

There was a sudden **scuffle**, a sound of blows, and out burst Abraham Gray with a knife cut on the side of the cheek. He came running to the captain, like a dog to the whistle.

"I'm with you, sir," said he.

And the next moment, all of us left the ship and jumped into a little rowboat. We sailed until we could see the stockade, and there, to our horror, were the five rogues. It flashed into my mind that

RASCAL (<u>rass</u> kuhl) *n.*
a dishonest, mean person
Synonyms: trickster, delinquent

STOOP (stoop) *v.* **-ing, -ed**
to crouch down
Synonyms: bend, duck

the ammunition and the powder for the gun had been left behind.

At great risk, we headed the boat to a landing place. Meanwhile, I could hear as well as see that **rascal**, Israel Hands, firing at us from the deck of the *Hispaniola*.

"Who's the best shot?" asked the captain.

"Mr. Trelawney, out and away," said I.

"Mr. Trelawney, will you please shoot one of these men, sir? Hands, if possible," said the captain.

Trelawney was as cool as steel. He made his pistol ready to shoot.

The squire raised his gun, the rowing stopped, and we leaned over to the other side to keep the boat balanced.

Just as Trelawney fired, the pirate **stooped**, the ball whistled over him, and felled one of the other men. The cry he gave was repeated not only by his companions on board but by a great number of voices from the shore. Looking in that direction I saw the other pirates running out from among the trees and tumbling into their places in the boats.

PACE (payss) *n.*
the speed someone or something is moving
Synonyms: time, rate

WADE (wayd) *v.* **-ing, -ed**
to walk through water
Synonyms: tread, plod

CONCERN (kon <u>sern</u>) *n.*
a feeling of anxiousness
Synonyms: worry, nervousness

"If we can't get ashore, we're in trouble," said the Captain.

"Only one of the boats is being manned, sir," I added, "The crew of the other is most likely going round by shore to cut us off."

In the meantime, we had been sailing at a good **pace** for a boat so heavy with supplies, and we had only taken on a little seawater in the boat.

The boat slowed, quite gently, in three feet of water. So far there was no great harm. No lives were lost, and we could **wade** ashore in safety.

But all our supplies were at the bottom of the boat, wet from the seawater. To make things worse, only two of our guns out of five were in good working order.

To add to our **concern**, we heard voices already drawing near us in the woods along the shore. We rushed ashore as fast as we could, leaving behind us the poor little boat and a good half of all our powder.

At every step we took, the voices of the buccaneers rang nearer. Soon we could hear their steps as they ran.

HESITATION (hez uh <u>tay</u> shun) *n.*
to pause or stop before doing something
Synonyms: waiting, delaying

ARRANGEMENT (uh <u>range</u> ment) *n.*
preparation
Synonym: plan

"Captain," said I, "Trelawney is the best shot. Give him your gun. His own is useless."

They exchanged guns. At the same time, observing Gray to be unarmed, I handed him my cutlass. Forty paces farther we came to the edge of the wood and saw the stockade in front of us. Almost at the same time, seven mutineers appeared in full cry at the southwestern corner.

They paused, and then we had time to fire at them. The four shots came in a scattering volley, but one of the enemy fell, and the rest, without **hesitation**, turned and plunged into the trees.

Just at that moment a pistol sounded in the bush, a ball whistled close past my ear, and poor Tom Redruth fell dead.

Then the Captain pulled me aside. "Dr. Livesey," he said, "When do you expect a ship to come and find us if we do not return?"

I told him it could be months. I had made **arrangements** for a rescue ship to come search for us if we did not return by a certain time. But that was the end of August, which meant many months before anyone even began to look for us.

RATIONS (<u>rah</u> shuns) *n.*
the amount of food or clothing set aside for an activity
Synonym: supplies

DESCEND (duh <u>send</u>) *v.* **-ing, -ed**
to come or go down
Synonyms: drop, decline

INVISIBLE (in <u>viz</u> uh buhl) *adj.*
not able to be seen
Synonyms: hidden, concealed

"We have enough powder to shoot," said the captain. "But the **rations** are short, very short, so short, Dr. Livesey, that we're perhaps as well without that extra mouth." And he pointed to the dead body. I felt sick seeing it, and I turned my head away.

Just then, with a roar and a whistle, a shot passed high above the roof of the log-house and went far beyond us in the wood.

"Oho!" said the captain. "Keep trying! You've little enough powder already, my lads."

The pirates shot at us again, and this time their aim was better. The ball **descended** inside the stockade, scattering a cloud of sand but doing no further damage.

"Captain," said the squire, "the house is quite **invisible** from the ship. It must be the flag they are aiming at. Would it not be wiser to take it in?"

"Strike my colors!" cried the captain. "No, sir, not I!" We all agreed with him. We wanted to show our enemies that we hated them and that we did not fear the shots they were firing at us.

All through the evening the pirates kept

MISSION (<u>mish</u> shun) *n.*
   a plan of action
      Synonyms: task, operation

BOLD (bold) *adj.*
   not afraid of danger
      Synonyms: fearless, confident

firing at us. "There is one good thing about all this," observed the captain, "the wood in front of us is likely clear. Our supplies should be uncovered and easy for us to get. <u>Volunteers</u> need to go and bring in pork."

Gray and Hunter were the first to come forward. Well armed, they stole out of the stockade, but it proved a useless **mission**. The mutineers were **bolder** than we thought. For four or five of them were busy carrying off our supplies and wading out with them to one of the boats that lay close by, pulling an oar or so to hold her in place against the current. Silver was in command, and every man of them was now provided with a musket from some secret stock of their own.

Suddenly, we heard a sound. "Doctor! Squire! Captain! Hullo, Hunter, is that you?" came the cries.

And I ran to the door in time to see Jim Hawkins, safe and sound, come climbing over the stockade.

HALT (halt) *n.*
a full stop
Synonyms: standstill, freeze

CHAPTER 8

Jim Hawkins Takes Up the Tale Again

As soon as Ben Gunn saw the flag, he came to a **halt**, stopped me by the arm, and sat down.

"Now," said he, "there's your friends."

"I think it's the mutineers," I answered.

"Nobody comes here but pirates," he cried. "Silver wouldn't put up any flag but his own. That's your friends, ashore in the old stockade, that was made years and years ago by Flint, and Flint was afraid only of Silver."

PURSUE (per <u>soo</u>) *v.* **-ing**, **-ed**
    to follow or go after
        Synonyms: chase, hound

PEAK (peek) *n.*
    the highest point of something
        Synonyms: top, apex

"Well," said I, "all the more reason that I should hurry on and join my friends."

"I won't go," said Ben, "not until I see one of your mates and gets it on his word of honor that I should be taken back and paid. And no one must know that Ben Gunn is here, or it will be the end of us. You just tell them I have reasons of my own for being here. And, Jim, if you was to see Silver, you wouldn't tell him about me, would you? Wild horses wouldn't draw it from you? No, says you!"

Here he was interrupted by a loud sound, and a cannonball came tearing through the trees and landed in the sand not a hundred yards from where we two were talking. The next moment each of us ran away in a different direction.

For a good hour cannon balls kept crashing through the woods. I moved from hiding-place to hiding-place, always **pursued**, or so it seemed to me, by these terrifying missiles.

The *Hispaniola* still lay where she had anchored. There, sure enough, was the black flag of the pirates, the Jolly Roger, flying from her **peak**. I watched all the action. Men were

DEMOLISH (duh <u>moll</u> ish) *v.* **-ing, -ed**
 to completely destroy
  Synonyms: tear down, obliterate

SENTRY (<u>sen</u> tree) *n.*
 a person who is standing watch
  Synonyms: watchman, guard

demolishing something with axes on the beach near the stockade. It was the poor little boat, I afterwards discovered. Away, near the river, a great fire was glowing among the trees, and between that point and the ship one of the gigs kept coming and going.

Then I ran through the woods until I had come back into the stockade and was soon warmly welcomed by the faithful party. I quickly told my story.

If we had been allowed to sit and do nothing, we should all have become blue, but Captain Smollett was never the man for that. All hands were called up before him, and he divided us into <u>watches</u>. The doctor and Gray and I were one. The squire, Hunter, and Joyce were the other. Tired though we all were, two were sent out for firewood, two more were set to dig a grave for Redruth. The doctor was named cook. I was the **sentry** at the door, and the captain himself went from one to another, keeping up our spirits and helping out.

From time to time the doctor came to the door for a little air and to rest his eyes, and whenever he

SANE (sane) *adj.*
not crazy; reasonable or sensible
Synonyms: all there, level-headed

PROSPECT (<u>pross</u> pek) *n.*
what might happen in the time to come
Synonyms: future, possibilities

did so, he had a word for me. "That man Smollett," he said once, "is a better man than I am."

Another time he came and was silent for a while. Then he put his head on one side, and looked at me.

"Is this Ben Gunn to be trusted?" he asked.

"I do not know, sir," said I. "I am not very sure whether he's **sane**."

"Well," returned the doctor. "A man who has been three years biting his nails on a desert island, Jim, can't expect to appear as sane as you or me. It doesn't lie in human nature."

Before supper was eaten, we buried old Tom in the sand and stood round him for a while in the breeze. A good deal of firewood had been gathered, but the captain did not think we had gathered enough. He shook his head and told us that we must gather even more tomorrow. Then, when we had eaten our pork, the three chiefs got together in a corner to discuss our **prospects**.

It appears they were at their wits' end what to do, the stores being so low that we must have been starved into surrender long before help came.

HAUL (hall) *v.* **-ing, -ed**
   to carry or drag
      Synonyms: remove, hoist

TRUCE (trooce) *n.*
   an agreement to stop fighting for a set time
      Synonyms: peace, reprieve

But our best hope, it was decided, was to kill off the buccaneers until they either **hauled** down their flag or ran away with the *Hispaniola*. From nineteen they were already now just fifteen. Two others were wounded, at least one severely, if he were not dead already. Every time we had a chance to take a crack at them, our chiefs decided, we were to take it.

"So," Trelawney declared, "They'll try to shoot us all down first, and then they'll try to get the schooner. With a ship, they can get to buccaneering again, I suppose."

"First ship that ever I lost," said Captain Smollett.

I was dead tired, and when I got to sleep, I slept like a log of wood. I was wakened by the sound of voices.

"Flag of **truce**!" I heard someone say. Then, immediately after, came cry of surprise, "Why, it's Silver himself!"

And at that, up I jumped, and rubbing my eyes, ran to a loophole in the wall.

Sure enough, there were two men just outside

TREACHEROUS (<u>trech</u> ur uhss) *adj.*
  done in a dishonest way
    Synonyms: deceitful, sneaky

TERM (turm) *n.*
  a point of an agreement
    Synonyms: condition, stipulation

PROMOTION (pruh <u>mo</u> shun) *n.*
  a move up to a higher level in a job
    Synonyms: advancement, step up

the stockade, one of them waving a white cloth, the other, Silver himself, standing by.

"Keep indoors, men," said the captain. "Ten to one this is a trick."

Then he hailed the buccaneer.

"Who goes? Stand, or we fire."

"Flag of truce," cried Silver.

The captain was on the porch, keeping himself carefully out of the way of a **treacherous** shot, should any be intended.

The captain turned and spoke to us, "Doctor's watch on the lookout. Dr. Livesey take the north side, if you please. Jim, the east. Gray, west. The watch below, all hands to load muskets. Quickly, men, and be careful."

And then he turned again to the mutineers.

"And what do you want with your flag of truce?" he cried.

"Cap'n Silver, sir, to come on board and make **terms**," he shouted.

"Cap'n Silver! My heart, and here's a **promotion**! When were you made a captain?"

DESERTION (duh <u>sur</u> shun) *n.*
leaving a task or position without permission
and with no thought of coming back
Synonyms: abandonment, withdrawal

EMPHASIS (<u>em</u> fuh siss) *n.*
the giving of special importance
Synonyms: attention, significance

SUBMIT(sub <u>mitt</u>) *v.* **-ing, -ed**
to give in to someone or something else
Synonyms: surrender, comply

Long John answered for himself. "These poor lads have chosen me captain. They did it only after your **desertion**, sir! "He lay an **emphasis** upon the word "desertion."

"We're willing to **submit**," came Silver's reply, "if we can come to terms. All I ask is your word, Cap'n Smollett, to let me safe and sound out of this here stockade, and one minute to get out of the path of your shot before a gun is fired."

"My man," said Captain Smollett, "if you wish to talk to me, you can come, that's all. If there's any treachery, it'll be on your side."

"That's enough, captain," shouted Long John cheerily. "A word from you's enough."

Silver came over to the stockade, threw over his crutch, got a leg up, and got himself over the fence and dropped safely to the other side.

I was far too much taken up with what was going on to be of any use as sentry. Indeed, I had already deserted my loophole and crept up behind the captain, who had now seated himself on the ground.

Silver at last arrived before the captain, whom

INKLING (<u>ingk</u> ling) *n.*
   a slight understanding
      Synonyms: hint, suspicion

GLEE (glee) *n.*
   happiness; open delight
      Synonyms: joy, elation

he saluted in the handsomest style, and then sat down beside him.

"Silver," said the captain, "if you had been an honest man, you might have been sitting in your galley, cooking and earning some money and being happy enough. This trouble is all your own doing. You're either my ship's cook, and then you are treated well, or you are Captain Silver, a common mutineer and pirate, and you can hang!"

"Well, now, you look here," said Silver. "One of my men was killed by you last night."

I began to have an **inkling**. Ben Gunn's last words came back to my mind. I began to think that Ben had paid the buccaneers a visit while they all lay drunk together round their fire, and he must have been the one to shoot Silver's man! I thought with **glee** that we now had only fourteen enemies to deal with.

"Well, here it is," said Silver. "We want that treasure! You want to save your lives. You have a chart, and we want it. I never meant you no harm, myself."

CLAP (klap) *v.* **-ing, -ed**
to place someone somewhere
Synonyms: hurl, toss

"We know exactly what you meant to do, and we don't care. Because now, you see, you can't do it," said the captain.

"Now," said Silver, "here it is. You give us the chart to get the treasure, and you stop shooting poor seamen while asleep. You do that, and we'll offer you a choice. Either you come aboard along of us, once the treasure is on the ship, and then I'll give you my word of honor to put you somewhere safe ashore. Or, if that ain't to your liking, because some of my men are rough, then you can stay here. We'll divide supplies with you and I'll give my word as to speak to the first ship I sight and send 'em here to pick you up."

Captain Smollett rose from his seat. "Is that all?" he asked.

"Refuse that, and you've seen the last of me but musket balls!" said Silver.

"Very good," said the captain. "Now you'll hear me. If you'll come up one by one, unarmed, I'll **clap** you all in irons and take you home to a fair trial in England. If you won't, I'll see you all to Davy Jones. You can't find the treasure. There's

WRATH (wrath) *n.*
strong anger
Synonyms: rage, vengeance

STUMBLE (<u>stum</u> buhl) *v.* **-ing, -ed**
to lose one's footing, to fall or almost fall
Synonyms: trip, stagger

INTERIOR (in <u>teer</u> ee ore) *n.*
the inner part
Synonym: inside

not a man among you fit to sail the ship. You can't fight us. I stand here and tell you so, and they're the last good words you'll get from me, for I'll put a bullet in your back when next I meet you."

Silver's eyes started in his head with **wrath**. Then he spat into the spring.

"There!" he cried. "That's what I think of you. Before an hour's out, I'll tear apart your old block house. Laugh, by thunder, laugh! Before an hour's out, you won't laugh because you will be dead! And them that die'll be the lucky ones."

And with an oath he **stumbled** off. As soon as Silver disappeared, the captain turned towards the **interior** of the house and found none of us at his post but Gray. It was the first time we had ever seen him angry.

"All of you get to your quarters!" he roared. We all went quickly back to our places.

"My lads," said the captain, "Before the hour's out, we shall be boarded by pirates. We're outnumbered, but I think we can beat them, if you choose. But not if you don't stand your posts and follow my orders!"

FEVER (<u>fee</u> vur) *n.*
  1. a state of heightened activity or excitement
     Synonyms: restlessness, frenzy
  2. a high body temperature
     Synonym: burning up

ENCLOSURE (en <u>kloz</u> shur) *n.*
  a space surrounded by nature, fence, or walls
     Synonyms: closed-in area, bounded area

On the two short sides of the house, east and west, there were only two loopholes to shoot through. There were two more on the south side, and five on the north side. There were muskets for the seven of us, and some ammunition. Four loaded muskets were soon laid ready.

"Doctor, you will take the door," the captain said. "Hunter, take the east side, there. Joyce, you stand by the west, my man. Mr. Trelawney, you are the best shot. You and Gray will take this long north side, with the five loopholes. That's where most of the danger is. If they can get up to it and fire in upon us through our own ports, things will begin to look bad for us. Hawkins, neither you nor I are much good at the shooting. We'll stand by to load the guns and help where we can."

We stood there, each at his post, in a **fever** of heat and anxiety. An hour passed away. And then suddenly Joyce whipped up his musket and fired. The sound had scarcely died away before it was repeated and repeated from outside in a scattering volley, shot behind shot, from every side of the **enclosure**. Several bullets struck the log-house, but

PRECISELY (pri <u>sisse</u> lee) *adv.*
in an exact way
Synonyms: definitely, absolutely

COMPUTATION (com pyu <u>tay</u> shun) *n.*
the act of figuring something out with math
or logic
Synonym: calculation

HOSTILITY (hoss <u>til</u> uh tee) *n.*
an act of war
Synonyms: fighting, aggression

not one entered. As the smoke cleared away and vanished, the stockade and the woods around it looked as quiet and empty as before.

"Did you hit your man?" asked the captain.

"No, sir," said Joyce. "I believe I did not, sir."

"Load his gun, Hawkins," ordered Captain Smollet. "How many would you say there were on your side, doctor?"

"I know **precisely**," said Dr. Livesey. "Three shots were fired on this side. I saw the three flashes – two close together – one farther to the west."

"Three!" repeated the captain. "And how many on yours, Mr. Trelawney?"

This was not so easily answered. There were seven shots from the north, by the squire's **computation**. Gray said there were eight or more. From the east and west, only a single shot had been fired. Because more shots had come from the north, it was plain to us that the attack would be from that direction. Only a small show of **hostilities** might come from all other directions.

But Captain Smollett made no change in his arrangements. If the mutineers succeeded in

SWARM (sworm) *v.* **-ing**, **-ed**
to move together in a group
Synonyms: rush, mob

crossing the stockade, he argued, they would take possession of any loophole they could and shoot us down like rats.

Suddenly, with a loud cry, a little group of pirates leaped from the woods on the north side and ran straight on the stockade. At the same moment, the fire was once more opened from the woods, and a bullet sang through the doorway and knocked the doctor's musket into bits.

The pirates **swarmed** over the fence. The squire and Gray fired again and yet again. Three pirates fell, one forwards into the enclosure, two back on the outside.

Two had died, one had fled, four entered close by us, while from the shelter of the woods seven or eight men, each supplied with several muskets, kept up a hot though useless fire on the log-house.

The four who had come close to us ran for the building, shouting as they ran, and the men among the trees shouted back. Several shots were fired. In a moment, the four pirates had swarmed up the mound and were upon us.

At the same moment, another pirate grabbed

CONFUSION (kuhn <u>fyu</u> shun) *n.*
a state of being without order
   Synonyms: chaos, commotion, disorder

Hunter's musket by the <u>muzzle</u> and pulled it through the loophole. With one blow, he knocked poor Hunter senseless on the floor. Meanwhile a third, running unharmed all around the outside of the house, appeared suddenly in the doorway and, with his cutlass, fell upon the doctor.

The log-house was full of smoke, which hid us and made us feel safer from the pirates. There was much **confusion**, though, and many cries. The flashes of pistol shots and one loud groan rang in my ears. Never had I felt more terrified about what might happen next.

"Out, lads, out, and fight 'em in the open! Cutlasses!" cried the captain.

I grabbed a cutlass from the pile, and ran out of the door into the clear sunlight. Someone was close behind.

"Round the house, lads!" cried the captain. Then I heard a change in his voice.

I turned eastwards, and with my cutlass raised, ran round the corner of the house. But soon the fight was over, and the victory was ours.

Of the four pirates who had attacked us, only

CLAMBER (klam bur) *v.* **-ing**, **-ed**
to climb on hands and feet with difficulty
Synonyms: crawl, scramble

SURVIVOR (sur <u>vye</u> vurs) *n.*
someone who remains alive after a difficult experience
Synonym: remaining one

STUNNED (stuhned) *adj.*
without awareness
Synonym: shocked senseless

one seemed a danger to us still. But maybe not, because this pirate was now **clambering** out again and running away.

"Fire – fire from the house!" cried the doctor. "And you, lads, back into cover."

In three seconds nothing remained of the attacking party but the five who had fallen.

The doctor and Gray and I ran full speed for shelter. The **survivors** would soon be back where they had left their muskets, and at any moment the fire might start up again.

The house was somewhat cleared of smoke, and we saw at a glance the price we had paid for victory. Hunter lay beside his loophole, **stunned**. Joyce was shot through the head. The squire was holding the captain, and both of them were pale.

"The captain's wounded," said Mr. Trelawney.

"All that could, have run," said the doctor, "but there's some of them will never run again."

"That means five left!" cried the captain. "Five against three is better odds than we had at start-ing. We were seven to nineteen then, or thought we were."

GRIEVOUS (<u>gree</u> vuhs) *adj.*
terrible or deadly
Synonyms: painful, agonizing

RECOVER (ri <u>kuhv</u> ur) *v.* **-ing, -ed**
to get better or become well
Synonyms: improve, heal

CONSULTATION (kon suhl <u>tay</u> shuhn) *n.*
a meeting between two or more people at
which matters are discussed
Synonym: conversation

CHAPTER 9

There was no return of the mutineers. Out of the eight men who had fallen in the action, only three still breathed. The pirate who had been shot at the loophole and Hunter both died. As for the captain, his wounds were **grievous** indeed, but not fatal. Anderson the pirate was sure to **recover**, but for weeks to come he must not walk nor move his arm nor even speak if he could help it.

After dinner the squire and the doctor sat by the captain's side awhile in **consultation**. When

ENVY (<u>en</u> vee) *v.* **-ing, -ed**
to want or wish to have something another
person has
Synonyms: covet, to be jealous

ESCAPADE (<u>ess</u> kuh pade) *n.*
a great adventure
Synonyms: undertaking, dangerous venture

SCHEME (skeem) *n.*
an organized plan of action
Synonyms: plot, game plan, strategy

they had talked to their hearts' content, then the doctor took up his hat and pistols, took a cutlass, put the chart in his pocket, and with a musket over his shoulder set off through the trees.

I knew he was going to meet with Ben. I began to **envy** him being out in the cool forest while I was stuck here in the ship's heat, and that evening, I took the first step towards my own **escapade**. I filled both pockets of my coat with biscuit and took a pistol and <u>powder horn</u> and bullets with me.

I had a **scheme** in my head. I was to go down the sandy area by the open sea and find a white rock I had seen last evening. I wanted to discover whether that was the white rock where Ben Gunn said he had hidden his boat. It was a thing quite worth doing, as I still believe. But as I was certain I should not be allowed to leave the enclosure, my only plan was to slip out when nobody was watching. I knew this was not a good plan, and that I should not leave my mates. But I was only a boy, and I had made my mind up.

Soon, I found a chance. The squire and Gray

PROPULSION (pruh <u>puhl</u> shun) *n.*
the process of moving something forward
Synonyms: power, movement

PREVENT (pruh <u>vent</u>) *v.* **-ing**, **-ed**
to keep from happening
Synonyms: block, stop

were busy helping the captain with his bandages. The coast was clear, and I made a run for it over the stockade and into the thickest of the trees.

Then I saw the *Hispaniola,* the Jolly Roger hanging from her peak. Just about the same time, the sun had gone down behind Spy-Glass Hill, and it began to grow dark. I saw I must lose no time if I were to find the boat that evening.

I could see the white rock, but it was still about an eighth of a mile further away. Night had almost come when I dropped into the hollow, lifted the side of the tent, and there was Ben Gunn's boat. The thing was very small, even for me. But it had a double paddle for **propulsion**.

My next plan was to slip out under cover of the night, cut the *Hispaniola* adrift, and let her go ashore. I had quite made up my mind that the mutineers wanted nothing more than to get away to sea. This, I thought, it would be a fine thing to **prevent**. And now that I had seen how they left their watchmen without a boat, I thought it might be done with little risk.

Down I sat to wait for darkness and made a

BLUR (blurr) *n.*
>something that cannot be seen clearly
>>Synonyms: smudge, fuzz

INDICATE (<u>in</u> duh kate) *v.* **-ing, -ed**
>to point out or show
>>Synonyms: announce, mark, reveal

LOOM (loom) *v.* **-ing, -ed**
>to appear in a sudden or terrifying way
>>Synonyms: approach, hover, emerge

STRAND (strand) *n.*
>one of the many threads twisted together to
>make a rope
>>Synonym: fiber

meal of biscuit. Then, I shouldered the little boat and made my way out of the hollow.

I could see the great fire on shore, where the pirates were warming themselves. I could also see a mere **blur** of light, **indicating** the position of the anchored ship. She had swung round, and the only lights on board were in the cabin.

The *Hispaniola* **loomed** before me. I got alongside her and laid hold of the tight rope that anchored her. The current was strong. One cut and the *Hispaniola* would go humming down the tide, but I worried the force of letting her go might drown me.

Suddenly, I heard the sound of loud, angry voices from the cabin. That made me make my mind up, and I took out my knife and cut one **strand** after another, till the vessel swung free.

I was almost instantly swept against the bows of the *Hispaniola*. I expected every moment to be drowned.

By this time both the schooner and my little boat were gliding pretty swiftly through the water. I wondered why the watchman aboard

WRESTLE (<u>ress</u> uhl) *n.*
a fight in which one grabs hold of one's
opponent and tries to throw them to the ground
Synonyms: struggle, battle

DISASTER (duh zass tur) *n.*
an event that ends in death, great damage
or pain
Synonyms: tragedy, catastrophe, ruin

the *Hispaniola* had taken no alarm. I looked up at the window in the ship and suddenly saw Hands and a companion locked together in a deadly **wrestle**, each with a hand upon the other's throat.

I began to hear the group on shore, as well. They were around the campfire and they had broken into the chorus I had heard so often: "Fifteen men on the dead man's chest! Yo-ho-ho, and a bottle of rum! Drink and the devil had done for the rest! Yo-ho-ho, and a bottle of rum!"

Suddenly the boat seemed to change her course. I glanced over my shoulder, and my heart jumped against my ribs. There, right behind me, was the glow of the camp-fire. The current was sweeping both the tall schooner and my little boat to the open sea! Finally, those on aboard the schooner took notice. One shout followed another on board. I could hear feet pounding and I knew that the two drunken pirates had at last been interrupted and awakened to a sense of their **disaster**.

I lay down flat in the bottom of that wretched

MIDST (midst) *n.*
the middle something
Synonyms: center, core

REPETITION (rep uh <u>tish</u> uhn) *n.*
the process of happening over and over again
Synonyms: duplication, recurrence

boat. I must have lain for hours, never ceasing to expect death at the next plunge. Gradually weariness grew upon me, even in the **midst** of my terrors, until sleep at last came, and I dreamed of home.

It was daylight when I awoke and found myself tossing at the southwest end of Treasure Island. It was my first thought to paddle in and land my little, light boat.

I saw the trees and then I saw another sight, that made me shiver. Right in front of me, not half a mile away, I saw the *Hispaniola.* I thought the pirates had sighted me and were trying to chase and catch me. At last, however, the boat stopped and stayed still, seeming to be almost helpless.

Again and again was this repeated. To and fro, up and down, north, south, east, and west, the *Hispaniola* sailed and then stopped. Each **repetition** ended as it had begun, with idly flapping sails. It became plain to me that nobody was steering the ship. But if this were so, where were the men? Either they were dead drunk, or they had deserted the ship, If they had deserted, I

INSPIRE (in <u>spire</u>) *v.* **-ing, -ed**
   to influence someone to want to do something
   or be like someone
      Synonyms: encourage, influence

REVOLVE (ruh <u>volv</u>) *v.* **-ing, -ed**
   to turn in a circular motion
      Synonyms: spin, rotate

thought, and if I could get on board I might return the vessel to her captain.

The current was strong. If only I dared to sit up and paddle, I knew I could reach the schooner. The scheme had an air of adventure that **inspired** me.

I got up and, with all my strength, paddled after the *Hispaniola*. I was now gaining rapidly on the schooner. I thought she was deserted. If not, the men were lying drunk below, where I might capture them and do what I chose with the ship.

At last, I had my chance. The breeze fell for some seconds, very low, and the current gradually turned the *Hispaniola* around. The ship **revolved** slowly and at last showed me her stern, with the cabin window still open. There was a wood beam overhead that I could grab onto.

I sprang to my feet and leaped. With one hand I caught the beam, and then I climbed aboard on the *Hispaniola*.

PROPPED (propped) *adj.*
   held up by leaning against something
      Synonyms: supported, braced

VICIOUS (<u>vish</u> uhss) *adj.*
   evil or cruel
      Synonyms: nasty, ferocious

CHAPTER 10

No one was to be seen. The planks, which had not been washed since the mutiny, were covered with footprints.

I saw the two watchmen. Redcap was on his back, dead and stiff. Israel Hands was **propped** up, his chin on his chest.

For a while the ship kept bucking like a **vicious** horse.

At the same time, I saw splashes of dark blood upon the planks and began to feel sure that they had killed each other.

WRITHE (wryth) *v.* **-ing**, **-ed**
    to twist and turn, usually in pain
        Synonyms: bend, contort

UTTER (<u>uh</u> ter) *v.* **-ing**, **-ed**
    to say something
        Synonyms: speak, express

While I was looking and wondering, Israel Hands turned partly round and with a low moan **writhed** himself back to the position in which I had seen him first. I walked until I reached the mainmast.

"I am here, Mr. Hands," I said.

He rolled his eyes round heavily, but he was too far gone to express surprise. All he could do was to **utter** one word, "Drink."

It occurred to me there was no time to lose, and I slipped down the stairs and below deck into the cabin to fetch him some water.

Everything was in confusion. All the locked places had been broken open in quest of the chart. Looking about, I found some water, some biscuit, some pickled fruits, a great bunch of raisins, and a piece of cheese. With these I came on deck to Israel. "Are you much hurt?" I asked.

"If that doctor was aboard," Israel said, "I'd be right enough, but I don't have any luck, you see. Where have you have come from?"

"Well," said I, "I've come aboard to take possession of this ship, Mr. Hands. And

you'll please regard me as your captain until further notice."

He looked at me sourly enough but said nothing. Some of the color had come back into his cheeks.

I ran to cut down the Jolly Roger flag. I waved my cap. "And there's an end to Captain Silver!"

"Well, Cap'n Hawkins," said Israel, "You gives me food and drink and a old scarf to tie my wound up, and I'll tell you how to sail the ship home. That makes us square all round, I take it."

"I'll tell you one thing," says I, "I'm not going back to Captain Kidd's cove where Silver is. I am going to get into North Inlet and beach the ship quietly there."

"I've tried my fling, I have, and I've lost," said Israel, "And it's you who is Captain!"

We struck our bargain on the spot. In three minutes I had the *Hispaniola* sailing easily before the wind along the coast of Treasure Island. I wanted to get to the North Inlet

PERMIT (per <u>mitt</u>) *v.* **-ing, -ed**
to give permission to do something
Synonyms: allow, enable

CONSCIENCE (<u>kon</u> shuhnss) *n.*
a source of moral judgment, that which helps
one judge between right and wrong
Synonyms: morals, scruples

CONQUEST (<u>kon</u> kwest) *n.*
something won by force
Synonyms: victory, success

where we might beach her safely until the tide **permitted** us to land.

Then I went below got a soft silk handkerchief. With this, and with my help, Hands bound up the great bleeding stab he had received in the <u>thigh</u>. After he had eaten a little and had a swallow or two more to drink, he began to pick up visibly.

The breeze was perfect for sailing. I was happy with my new command, and pleased with the bright, sunshiny weather. I had now plenty of water and good things to eat, and my **conscience**, which had hit me hard for my desertion, was quieted by the great **conquest** I had made. The eyes of Israel Hands followed me as I walked about the deck. There was an odd smile, too, on his face. It was a smile that had in it something both of pain and weakness. But there was also a shadow of treachery in his expression as he watched and watched and watched me at my work.

With Hands's help, we sailed to shore. His eyes never met mine. They kept wandering to and fro, up and down. All the time he kept smiling and

DECEPTION (di <u>sep</u> shun) *n.*
a falsehood or lie
Synonyms: cheat, scam

CONFIRM (kon <u>firm</u>) *v.* **-ing**, **-ed**
to make sure something thought true is true
Synonyms: check, verify

THRUST (thrust) *v.* **-ing**, **-ed**
to push violently forward
Synonym: stab

VICTIM (<u>vik</u> tuhm) *n.*
a person who is hurt or killed
Synonyms: hunted, prey

putting his tongue out, so that a child could have told that he was bent on some **deception**. "I wonder if you could get me some more water from down below?" he asked.

I knew he wanted me below deck so he could do some mischief, but I knew, too, that my guns were below as well. With that I ran down to another place where I could come on board, watch him, and he would not see me.

What I saw **confirmed** my suspicions. In half a minute he had pulled a long knife out from a pile of rope. He looked upon it for a moment, **thrusting** forth his lower jaw, tried the point upon his hand, and then, quickly concealing it in his jacket, hurried back again into his old place against the <u>bulwark.</u>

This was all that I needed to know. Israel could move about, he was now armed, and if he had been at so much trouble to get rid of me, it was plain that I was meant to be the **victim**.

Yet I felt we were still joined in wanting one thing. We both wanted to have the schooner safe, so that, when the time came, she could be sent off

PERIL (<u>per</u> uhl) *n.*
   great danger
      Synonyms: uncertainty, jeopardy

FURY (<u>fyur</u> ee) *n.*
   uncontrolled and wild anger
      Synonyms: rage, ferocity

to sail again with as little work and danger as possible. And until that was done I considered that my life would be spared.

Hands gave me directions to guide the ship to shore, and I followed them to the letter until the *Hispaniola* swung round rapidly and aimed for the low, wooded shore.

In the excitement of the landing, I had quite forgot the **peril** that hung over my head. When I looked round, there was Hands, already halfway towards me, with the knife in his right hand.

We must both have cried out aloud when our eyes met, but while mine was the cry of terror, his was a roar of **fury** like a charging bull's. At the same instant, he threw himself forward and I leapt sideways towards the ship's bow. As I did so, I let go of the <u>tiller</u>, and I think this saved my life, for it struck Hands across the chest and stopped him, for the moment, dead.

Before he could recover, I was safe out of the corner where he had had me trapped. I stopped by the mainmast and pulled a pistol from my pocket, took a cool aim, though he had already

MAST (mast) *n.*
a pole that holds a sail on a ship
Synonym: spar

turned and was once more coming directly after me, and pulled the <u>trigger</u>. But the gun didn't work! I cursed myself. Why had I not reloaded my only weapons?

Wounded as he was, he moved fast, his hair tumbling over his face. I had no time to try my other pistol, but I was sure it would be useless.

I quickly got out of his way, and he followed after me. When he moved one way, I went the other. It was such a game as I had often played at home about the rocks of Black Hill Cove, but never before, you may be sure, with such a wildly beating heart as now. Still, as I say, it was a boy's game, and I thought I could hold my own at it against an old seaman with a wounded thigh. Well, while this game went on, suddenly the *Hispaniola* struck ground, in the sand, and both of us fell onto the deck.

I was the first on my feet. I ran to the top of the **mast**. Below me was Israel Hands, with his mouth open and his face upturned to mine. He was standing like a <u>statue</u>.

Now that I had a moment to myself, I lost no

PAINFULLY (<u>payne</u> fool ee) *adv.*
with agony or extreme discomfort
Synonym: agonizingly

PANG (pang) *n.*
a sharp physical discomfort
Synonyms: pain, ache

time in recharging my pistols. With the knife in his teeth, Hands began slowly and **painfully** to mount. It cost him no end of time and groans to pull his wounded leg behind him, and I had quietly finished my arrangements before he was much more than a third of the way up. Then, with a pistol in either hand, I called to him. "One more step, Mr. Hands," said I, "and I'll blow your brains out!"

He stopped instantly. All of a sudden, back went his right hand over his shoulder. Something sang like an arrow through the air. I felt a blow and then a sharp **pang**, and there I was pinned by the shoulder to the mast. In the horrid pain and surprise of the moment, both my pistols went off, and both escaped out of my hands. They did not fall alone. With a choked cry, Hands lost his grasp and fell head first into the water.

Hands rose to the surface in a <u>lather</u> of foam and blood and then sank again for good. I began to feel sick, faint, and terrified. The blood was running over my back and chest. The knife, where it had pinned my shoulder to the mast, seemed to

PLUCK (pluk) *v.* **-ing, -ed**
to remove by grabbing and pulling quickly
Synonyms: snatch, yank

SECURE (si <u>kyur</u>) *v.* **-ing, -ed**
to guard from danger
Synonyms: shelter, shield

burn like a hot iron, yet what I was most worried over was the horror I had of falling from the cross-trees into that still green water, beside the body of Israel Hands.

It was my first thought to **pluck** out the knife. I did so with a sudden jerk, and then I was able to climb down. I went below and did what I could for my wound. It pained me a good deal and still bled freely, but it was neither deep nor dangerous, nor did it bother me when I used my arm. Then I looked around me. The ship was now my own. I began to think of clearing it from its last passenger–the dead man, O'Brien, that Hands had been arguing with.

I was now alone upon the ship. The tide had just turned. I began to see a danger to the ship. I did what I could to **secure** the ship and make her safe. For the rest, the *Hispaniola* must trust to luck, like myself.

I looked over at the water. It seemed shallow enough, and holding a rope tied to the ship, I let myself drop softly overboard. The water reached my waist. The sand was firm, and I waded ashore

ACHIEVEMENT (uh <u>cheev</u> ment) *n.*
something done successfully
Synonyms: accomplishment, attainment

TRUANCY (<u>troo</u> uhn see) *n.*
failure to be present
Synonym: absence

RADIANCE (<u>ray</u> dee uhnce) *n.*
vivid light or brightness
Synonyms: glow, brilliance

in great spirits, leaving the *Hispaniola* on her side, with her mainsail trailing wide upon the surface of the bay, clear at last from buccaneers and ready for our own men to board and get to sea again. I wanted nothing more than to get home to the stockade and boast of my **achievements**. Possibly I might be blamed for my **truancy**, but the capture of the *Hispaniola* was a great deed, and I hoped that even Captain Smollett would approve.

So thinking, and in great spirits, I began to walk to the block house and my companions.

I walked toward where I had first met Ben Gunn. I saw a glow in the sky and thought it must be Ben cooking his supper before a fire. And yet I wondered, why he would be so careless. For if I could see this **radiance**, might it not reach the eyes of Silver himself where he camped upon the shore among the marshes?

And then, right in front of me a glow of a different color appeared among the trees. It was red and hot, like a <u>bonfire</u>.

For the life of me I could not think what it might be. At last I came to the clearing. The

CREEP (kreep) *v.* **-ing, -ed**
to move quietly and slowly
Synonyms: tiptoe, sneak

DISTINGUISH (diss <u>ting</u> gwish) *v.* **-ing, -ed**
to recognize or see details
Synonyms: identify, make out

blockhouse itself, still lay in a black shadow. There was not a person stirring, nor was there a sound beside the noises of the breeze.

I stopped, with much wonder in my heart, and perhaps a little terror also. It had not been our way to build great fires, and I began to fear that something had gone wrong while I was gone.

I stole round by the eastern end, keeping close in shadow. I got upon my hands and knees and crawled, without a sound, towards the corner of the house. As I drew nearer, I was delighted to hear my friends <u>snoring</u> together in their sleep.

In the meantime, there was no doubt of one thing. They kept a very bad watch. If it had been Silver and his lads that were now **creeping** in on them, no one would have seen daybreak. If the captain hadn't been wounded, I thought the watch would have been better. I blamed myself sharply for leaving them in that danger with so few to do guard duty.

By this time I had got to the door and stood up. All was dark within, so that I could **distinguish** nothing. I walked steadily in. I should lie down

ARRIVAL (uh <u>rye</u> vuhl) *n.*
the act of reaching a place
Synonyms: entrance, appearance

RECOIL (rih <u>koyle</u>) *v.* **-ing, -ed**
to pull back in fear or disgust
Synonyms: turn away, shrink

BRAND (brand) *n.*
1. a piece of wood that is lit on fire
Synonym: torch
2. a sign or name telling who made the product
Synonyms: label, logo

in my own place (I thought with a silent chuckle) and enjoy their faces when they found me in the morning.

And then, all of a sudden, a shrill voice broke forth out of the darkness:

"Pieces of eight! Pieces of eight! Pieces of eight! Pieces of eight! Pieces of eight!" and so forth, without pause or change.

It was Silver's green parrot, Captain Flint! She was keeping better watch than any human being, announcing my **arrival** with her screaming.

At the scream of the parrot, the sleepers awoke and sprang up. And with a mighty oath, the voice of Silver cried, "Who goes?"

I turned to run, struck against one person, **recoiled**, and ran full into the arms of a second, who held me tight.

"Bring a torch, Dick," said Silver. "This lad has been captured!"

One of the men left the log-house and returned with a lighted **brand**.

APPREHENSION (<u>ap</u> pre <u>hen</u> shun) *n.*
   a fearful state
      Synonyms: worry, uneasiness, dread

PERISH (peh <u>rish)</u> *v.* **-ing, -ed**
   to lose one's life, especially by murder, sudden
   illness, or accident
      Synonyms: die, expire

CHAPTER 11

The red glare of the torch lit up the inside of the block house. My worst **apprehensions** were realized. The pirates were in possession of the house and stores. I could only think that all had **perished**, and if I had been there, I would have perished with them. There were six of the buccaneers, all told, not another man was left alive. Five of them were on their feet.

The parrot sat on Long John's shoulder. He himself, I thought, looked somewhat paler and more stern than I was used to. "So," said he, "here's

SCAMP (skamp) *n.*
> a young person who misbehaves or disobeys
>> Synonyms: imp, brat, rascal

INCENSED (in <u>senssed</u>) *adj.*
> extremely angry
>> Synonyms: enraged, furious

DISTRESSED (dis <u>tresd</u>) *adj.*
> to have a worried state of mind
>> Synonyms: upset, anxious, concerned

GRACIOUS (<u>gray</u> shuss) *adj.*
> having grace or politeness
>> Synonyms: goodhearted, courteous

Jim Hawkins, <u>shiver my timbers</u>! Well, come, I take that friendly. I see you were smart when first I set my eyes on you. I always wanted you to join us and take your share, and now, you have no choice but to join us. Your friends won't have you. 'Ungrateful **scamp**' was what the doctor called you."

My friends, then, were still alive, and though I partly believed the truth of Silver's statement, that they were **incensed** at me for my desertion, I was more relieved than **distressed** by what I heard.

"Well," says I, growing a bit bolder, "if I'm to choose, I declare I have a right to know what's what, and why you're here, and where my friends are."

And then, in his first **gracious** tones, he replied to me, "Yesterday morning, Mr. Hawkins," said he, "Doctor Livesey came with a flag of truce. Says he, 'Cap'n Silver, you're sold out. Ship's gone.' We looked out, and by thunder, the old ship was gone! 'Well,' says the doctor, 'let's bargain.' We bargained, him and I, and here we are. We have supplies, the blockhouse, the firewood you was thoughtful enough to cut, and in a manner of speaking, the whole blessed boat. As for them, they've vanished."

LEST (lesst) *conj.*
done in hopes of avoiding something
unpleasant
Synonym: unless

TREATY (<u>treet</u> tee) *n.*
an agreement between two parties, often
ending a conflict of some kind
Synonyms: deal, pact

He took one long, deep breath. "And **lest** you should take it into that head of yours," he went on, "that you was included in the **treaty**, here's the last word that was said: 'How many are you,' says I, 'to leave?' 'Four,' says he; 'four, and one of us wounded. As for that boy, I don't know where he is,' says he, 'nor I don't much care.' And now you are to choose whether you shall join us," said Silver.

"Well," said I, "I now have something to tell you. Here you are, in a bad way. Your ship is lost, your treasure is lost, your men are lost, and your whole business has gone to wreck! And if you want to know who did it – it was I! I was in the apple barrel the night we sighted land, and I heard you, John, and you, Dick Johnson, and Hands, who is now at the bottom of the sea, and told every word you said before the hour was out. And as for the schooner, it was I who cut her <u>cable</u>, and it was I that killed the men you had aboard of her, and it was I who brought her where you'll never see her more, not one of you. Kill me, if you please, or spare me. But one thing I'll say, and no more. If you spare me, bygones are bygones, and when you fellows are in

WITNESS (<u>wit</u> ness) *n.*
someone who sees something happening
Synonyms: observer, testifier

GALLOWS (<u>gal</u> ohs) *n.*
the apparatus on which criminals are hanged
Synonyms: noose, gibbet

STEADY (<u>sted</u> ee) *adj.*
firmly in place, consistent
Synonyms: fixed, unfaltering

court for piracy, I'll try to save you. It is for you to choose. Kill another and do yourselves no good, or spare me and keep a **witness** to save you from the **gallows**."

I stopped, for I was out of breath, and to my wonder, not a man of them moved, but all sat staring at me like sheep. I broke out again, "And now, Mr. Silver," I said, "I believe you're the best man here, and if things go to the worst, I'll take it kind of you to let the doctor know the way I took it."

"I'll bear it in mind," said Silver.

The men began to argue about me and Silver spoke out. "I like that boy. I never seen a better boy than that. He's more a man than any pair of rats of you in this here house, and what I say is this: no one must lay a hand to him!" The men silenced and soon left Silver and me alone.

"Now, look you here, Jim Hawkins," Silver said in a **steady** whisper. "They could kill you. But, I will save you if you will help save me!"

"You are desperate because you think that all's lost?" I asked.

"Aye, by gum, I do think that!" he answered.

HOBBLE (<u>hob</u> buhl) *v.* **-ing**, **-ed**
  to walk awkwardly or limp
    Synonyms: stagger, stumble

CONSPIRATOR (kon <u>spir</u> uh ter) *n.*
  one who plans secretly with others, usually to
  do something wrong or illegal
    Synonyms: associate, accomplice,
    confederate

"Once I looked into that bay, Jim Hawkins, and seen no schooner, I gave up. As for the pirates and their council, mark me, they're fools and cowards. I'll save your life if I can. But, see here, Jim, you save Long John from swinging from the gallows."

"What I can do, that I'll do," I said.

"It's a bargain!" cried Long John. "You speak up for me if the time comes, and I've a chance!"

He **hobbled** to the torch and took a fresh light to his pipe.

"Understand me, Jim," he said, returning. "I'm on the squire's side now. I know the pirates will turn on me, and I know you've got that ship safe somewheres. How you done it, I don't know, but safe it is. But what I don't understand, and maybe you do, is why the doctor give me the treasure chart!" I looked at him in wonder.

"There's some reason for it," Silver said. "Good or bad, we don't know." And he shook his great fair head like a man who looks forward to the worst.

The council of buccaneers had lasted some time. I turned to the loophole nearest me and looked out. The **conspirators** stood around a torch. I saw

HUDDLED (<u>hud</u> uhld) *adj.*
closely or tightly gathered together in a group
Synonyms: packed, crammed

RETORT (ri <u>tort</u>) *v.* **-ing, -ed**
to answer quickly
Synonyms: respond, counter, rejoin

the blade of an open knife shine in the torchlight. The whole party began to move together towards the house.

"Here they come," said I.

"Well, let 'em come, lad! Let 'em come," said Silver cheerily.

The door opened, and the five men, standing **huddled** together just inside, pushed one of their number forward who handed something to Silver.

Silver looked at what had been given him.

"The black spot! It says I'm no longer your captain!" he cried.

One of the pirates spoke, "We want you to step down, we do. You've made a mess of this cruise. You let the enemy out of this here trap for nothing. Third, you wouldn't let us kill them. And then, fourth, there's this here boy."

"Is that all?" asked Silver quietly.

"Enough, too," **retorted** another of the pirates. "We'll all hang because you made a mess of things."

"Well, now, look here," cried Silver. "I made

HOSTAGE (<u>hoss</u> tij) *n.*
someone taken and held by one group to make
sure another group will meet certain demands
Synonyms: prisoner, captive

a mess of things, did I? Well, now, you all know what I wanted, and you all know if that had been done that we'd have been aboard the *Hispaniola* this night as ever was, every man of us alive, and fit, and the treasure in the ship, too, by thunder! Well, who crossed me? Who forced my hand? Why, it was Anderson and Hands and you, George Merry!"

The other pirates looked suddenly uneasy.

"Well," said Silver. "As for that boy, why, shiver my timbers, isn't he a **hostage**? Are we a-going to waste a hostage? No, not us. He might be our last chance! And number three? Maybe you don't count it nothing to have a real doctor to see you every day? And maybe, perhaps, you didn't know there was another ship coming to get us if we don't return? But there is, and not so long till then. And we'll see who'll be glad to have a hostage when it comes to that."

And he threw down upon the floor a paper that I instantly recognized. It was none other than the chart on yellow paper, with the three red crosses, that I had found in the oilcloth at the

ACCOMPANY (uh <u>kum</u> puh nee) *v.* **-ing, -ed**
to go along with
Synonyms: join, coincide

REMARKABLE (ri <u>mar</u> kuh buhl) *adj.*
to be worth noticing or commenting upon
Synonyms: amazing, great, extraordinary

ENGAGED (en <u>gayjd</u>) *adj.*
1. busy doing something
Synonyms: involved, absorbed
2. committed to marry
Synonyms: promised, betrothed

bottom of the captain's chest. But why had the doctor given it to him?

The mutineers leaped upon it like cats upon a mouse. It went from hand to hand, one tearing it from another. There were so many oaths and cries and such laughter that **accompanied** their examination, you would have thought that they were holding the very gold in their hands.

Silver sprang up. "You lost the ship. I found the treasure!" he cried. "Who's the better man at that? And now I resign, by thunder! Elect whom you please to be your cap'n now. I'm done with it."

"Silver!" they cried. "We elect Silver!"

That was the end of the night's business. Soon after, we lay down to sleep. My mind was full of thoughts.

I kept thinking about the **remarkable** game Silver was now **engaged** in playing. He had to try to keep the mutineers together, but he also wanted to make his peace and save his miserable life. He slept peacefully and snored aloud, yet my heart was sore for him, wicked as he was, to think on the dark perils that awaited him.

STEALTHY (<u>stel</u> thee) *adj.*
secretive and quiet
Synonyms: sneaky, sly

ALTERATION (awl tur <u>ay</u> shun) *n.*
a change of form or manner
Synonyms: switch, modification

CHAPTER 12

We were all wakened by a voice hailing us from the woods: Here's the doctor."

I remembered my **stealthy** conduct, and I felt ashamed to look him in the face.

Dr. Livesey was by this time across the stockade and into the block house, and he looked surprised to see me. I could hear the **alteration** in his voice as he said, "Is that you, Jim?"

"The very same Jim as ever was," says Silver.

"Well, well," the doctor said at last, "duty

DEMON (<u>dee</u> muhn) *n.*
   devil or evil person
      Synonyms: villain, fiend

PROFESSIONAL (pruh <u>fesh</u> uh nuhl) *adj.*
   skilled in a certain field of work
      Synonyms: well-qualified, expert

PLEDGE (pledj) *n.*
   a promise to do something
      Synonyms: oath, vow

first and pleasure afterwards. Let us look at these patients of yours."

He gave me one nod and then went about his work among the sick. He must have known that his life, among these treacherous **demons**, depended on his staying on their good side. He talked to his patients as if he were paying an ordinary **professional** visit to a quiet English family.

"I am a mutineers' doctor, or prison doctor as I prefer to call it," says Doctor Livesey in his pleasantest way, "I make it a point of honor not to lose a man for the gallows."

"Si-lence!" Silver suddenly roared. "Doctor," he went on in his usual tones, "I was thinking. I know you had a fancy for the boy. We're all grateful for your kindness. And I take it I've found a way that might please all of us, that I'd like to talk to you about. Hawkins, will you give me your word of honor as a young gentleman not to run away?"

I readily gave the **pledge**.

"Then, doctor," said Silver, "you just step outside o' that stockade, and once you're there, I'll bring the boy down, too."

SACRIFICING (<u>sak</u> ruh fisse ing) *n.*
the act of giving something important up for
a reason
Synonyms: surrendering, parting with,
forfeiting

DELIBERATELY (duh <u>lib</u> ur uht lee) *adv.*
in a planned way
Synonyms: intentionally, purposefully,
consciously

Just as the doctor left the house, the other pirates began to shout. Silver was accused of **sacrificing** a hostage to earn favor for himself.

Very **deliberately**, Silver and I made our way across the sand, where the doctor waited for us on the other side of the stockade. As soon as we were there beside the doctor, Silver stopped.

"You'll make a note of this here also, doctor," he said. "And the boy'll tell you how I saved his life, and how because of it, the other men told me I was not Captain any more. You wouldn't think of helping me, too, would you?" Silver's voice trembled.

"Why, John, you're afraid?" asked Dr. Livesey.

"Doctor, I'm no coward," he said. "But I'll own up fairly, I'm afraid of the gallows. You're a good man. And you'll not forget what I done good, not any more than you'll forget the bad, I know. And I step aside and leave you and Jim alone. And you'll remember I did that good thing, won't you?"

So saying, he stepped back a little way, till he was out of earshot, and there sat down upon a tree-stump.

"So, Jim," said the doctor sadly, "here you are.

TORTURE (<u>tor</u> chur) *n.*
the act of causing horrible and deliberate pain
to make someone do something
Synonyms: persecution, torment

I cannot find it in my heart to blame you, but this much I will say. When Captain Smollett was well, you dared not have gone off; and when he was ill and couldn't help it, it was cowardly!"

"Doctor," I said, weeping. "I have blamed myself enough. I should have been dead by now if Silver hadn't stood up for me. And doctor, believe this, I can die, and I even say I deserve it, but what I fear is **torture**! If they torture me, I—"

"Jim," the doctor interrupted, and his voice was quite changed, "Jim, we'll run for it."

"Doctor," said I, "I gave my word."

"I know, I know," he cried. "One jump, and you're out, and we'll run for it like antelopes."

"No," I replied, "you know right well you wouldn't do that yourself, not you nor the squire nor captain. I won't do that, either. Silver trusted me. I gave my word, and back I go. But, doctor, you did not let me finish. If they come to torture me, I might let slip a word of where the ship is, for I got the ship, part by luck and part by risking. She lies in North Inlet, on the southern beach, and just below high water."

SQUALL (skwall) *n.*
A storm, usually bringing rain or snow
Synonym: tempest

"The ship!" exclaimed the doctor.

I described my adventures, and he heard me out in silence.

"There is a kind of fate in this," he said when I had done. "Every step, it's you that saves our lives. And do you think by any chance that we are going to let you lose yours? That would be a poor return, my boy. You found out what the pirates were up to. You found Ben Gunn."

Silver came suddenly near us. "Silver!" the doctor cried. "I'll give you a piece of advice. Don't you be in any great hurry after that treasure."

"But if I'm not, the other men will kill me," said Silver.

"Well, Silver," replied the doctor, "if that is so, I'll go one step further. Look out for **squalls** when you find it."

"Sir," said Silver, "between man to man, that's too much and too little. But I ask you, why did you leave the block house? Why did you give me that treasure chart?"

The doctor was quiet for a minute. "It's not my secret to tell, Silver," he said finally. "But, I'll give

CONCESSION (kon <u>sesh</u> uhn) *n.*
the act of giving up something
Synonyms: compromise, deal, trade-off

BRISK (brisk) *adj.*
done quickly
Synonyms: lively, fast, vigorous

GLINT (glint) *n.*
a small, bright flash of light
Synonyms: glimmer, gleam

you a bit of hope. Silver, if we both get out of here alive, I'll do my best to save you."

Silver's face was radiant. "You couldn't say more, sir, not if you was my mother," he cried.

"Well, that's my first **concession**," added the doctor. "My second is another piece of advice. Keep the boy close beside you, and when you need help, halloo. I'm off to seek help for you, and that should show you that I speak the truth. Good-bye, Jim."

Dr. Livesey shook hands with me through the stockade, nodded to Silver, and set off at a **brisk** pace into the wood.

"Jim," said Silver when we were alone, "if I saved your life, you saved mine, and I'll not forget it. I seen the doctor waving you to run for it and I seen you say no. This is the first **glint** of hope I had since the attack failed, and I owe it you. And now, Jim, we're to go in for this here treasure-hunting, and I don't like it. You and me must stick close, back to back, and we'll save our necks in spite of fate and fortune."

We all ate breakfast with the mates, and Silver

RESTORE (ri <u>stor</u>) *v.* **-ing, -ed**
to give or bring back
Synonyms: heal, mend, rebuild

HUMOR (<u>hyoo</u> mur) *n.*
1. the ability to laugh at things
Synonyms: fun, amusement
2. a state of mind
Synonyms: mood, temperament

SUSPICION (suss <u>pish</u> uhn) *n.*
having the thought that something is wrong
Synoyms: doubt, distrust, misgiving

became loud. "Aye, mates," said he, "it's lucky you have Barbecue to think for you with this here head. I got what I wanted, I did. Sure enough, they have the ship. Where they have it, I don't know yet, but once we hit the treasure, we'll take the ship for ourselves again. And we have a hostage."

He **restored** their hope and confidence, and repaired his own at the same time.

"I'll take the boy – our hostage – and tie him to me with rope, when we go treasure-hunting. We'll keep him like so much gold. Once we got the ship and treasure both and off to sea like companions, why then we'll give Mr. Hawkins back, we will, and we'll give him his share, to be sure, for all his kindness."

It was no wonder the men were in a good **humor** now. Silver was friendly to the pirates and friendly to us. There was no doubt he would prefer gold and freedom with the pirates to an escape from hanging, which was the best he had to hope for if he stayed on our side.

What danger lay before us! What a moment that would be when the **suspicions** of his

CAPTOR (<u>kap</u> tor) *n.*
someone who holds one by force
Synonyms: capturer, kidnapper

QUEST (kwest) *n.*
the act of searching for something
Synonyms: chase, hunt, mission

EQUIPPED (ih <u>kwippd</u>) *adj.*
given necessary or useful item
Synonyms: supplied, fitted

followers turned to certainty and he and I should have to fight for dear life, he a cripple and I a boy, against five strong and active seamen!

Add to this was the mystery that still hung over the way my friends were acting. There was their unexplained desertion of the stockade and their giving the chart to Silver. Harder still to understand, was the doctor's last warning to Silver, "Look out for squalls when you find it." I was so upset I couldn't eat my breakfast. It was with an uneasy heart that I set out behind my **captors** on the **quest** for treasure.

I had a line tied about my waist and followed after the cook, who held the loose end of the rope, now in his free hand, now between his teeth. For all the world, I was led like a dancing bear.

The other men were carrying picks and shovels that they had brought ashore from the *Hispaniola*. Some men were carrying pork, bread, and brandy for the <u>midday</u> meal. Thus **equipped**, we all set out to the beach, where the two boats awaited us. As we made our way, there was some talk about the chart and how best to find the

READING (reed ing) *n.*
1. data shown by a measuring instrument such as a meter or a compass
Synonym: information
2. the act of examining or studying
Synonyms: interpretation, examination

TETHERED (<u>teth</u> urd) *adj.*
tied up
Synonyms: bound, confined

treasure. The chart showed a tall tree, but which tall tree did it mean?

The top of the hill was dotted thickly with pine trees of all different sizes and shapes and heights. Every here and there you could find a different kind of tree rising forty or fifty feet clear above its neighbours. Which one of these could be the "tall tree" of Captain Flint could only be decided by the **readings** of the <u>compass</u>.

The party spread itself out, in a fan shape, shouting and leaping. About the center, and a good way behind the rest, Silver and I followed. I was **tethered** by my rope.

We had thus gone for about half a mile when the man upon the farthest left began to cry aloud, as if in terror. Shout after shout came from him, and the others began to run in his direction.

"He can't have found the treasure," said old Morgan, hurrying past us from the right, "for that's farther away."

Indeed, as we found when we also reached the spot, the man had found something very different. At the foot of a pine, a skeleton

NOTION (<u>no</u> shun) *n.*
an idea or a belief
Synonyms: thought, opinion

NUMBSKULL (<u>num</u> skull) *n.*
a brain that does not work well
Synonyms: dull brain, dim bulb

DULY (<u>doo</u> lee) *adv.*
in the correct way or time
Synonyms: appropriately, properly

lay. I believe a chill struck for a moment to every heart.

"He was a seaman," said George Merry, who, bolder than the rest, had gone up close and was looking at the rags of clothing. "This is good sea cloth."

"But what sort of a way is that for bones to lie? It isn't natural!" declared Silver.

The man lay perfectly straight, his feet pointing in one direction, his hands, raised above his head, pointing directly in the opposite.

"I've taken a **notion** into my old **numbskull**," observed Silver, taking up the map and compass. "This skeleton's a kind of compass! There's the tip-top point of Skeleton Island, stickin' out like a tooth. Just take a bearing, will you, along the line of them bones."

The body pointed straight in the direction of the island, and the compass read **duly** East Southeast and then East again.

We were all uneasy now. The pirates no longer ran shouting through the wood, but kept side by side and spoke quietly. The terror of the dead buccaneer had fallen on their spirits.

INCREASE (in <u>krees</u>) *v.* **-ing**, **-ed**
   to become larger in size
      Synonyms: add, augment

CHAPTER 13

There was no sound but that of the distant waves and the <u>chirp</u> of insects in the brush. Not a man, not a sail was upon the sea. The whole view **increased** the sense of solitude.

Silver, as he sat, studied his compass.

"There are three 'tall trees'" said he, "about in the right line from Skeleton Island. 'Spy-glass shoulder,' I take it, means that lower point there. It's child's play to find the stuff now."

All of a sudden, out of the middle of the trees

AFFECT (uh <u>fekt</u>) *v.* **-ing, -ed**
  to be moved emotionally
    Synonyms: influence, impact

COURAGEOUS (kuh <u>ray</u> juss) *adj.*
  being without fear
    Synonyms: brave, bold

WAIL (wale) *v.* **-ing, -ed**
  to make a long, high-pitched sound
    Synonyms: cry, howl, bawl

ROOT (root) *v.* **-ing, -ed**
  1. to stand motionless in fear or shock
    Synonym: frozen
  2. to be established or to be dug deeply into the ground
    Synonym: planted

in front of us, a thin, high, trembling voice struck up the well-known air and words:

"Fifteen men on the dead man's chest – Yo-ho-ho, and a bottle of rum!"

I never have seen men more **affected** than the pirates. The color went from their six faces. Some leaped to their feet. Some grabbed hold of others.

"It's Flint!" cried Merry.

The song had stopped as suddenly as it began. "No," said Silver, struggling to get the words out. "It's not Flint!"

His courage had come back as he spoke. Already the others were becoming more **courageous**, too.

Then, the same voice broke out again. "Darby M'Graw," it **wailed**. "Darby M'Graw! Darby M'Graw!" It wailed that name again and again and again. The buccaneers remained **rooted** to the ground. Long after the voice had died away, they still stared in silence.

"That fixes it!" gasped one. "Let's go."

"Those were Flint's last words," moaned Morgan, "His last words above board."

CHAT (chat) *v.* **-ing**, **-ed**
to discuss in a casual, informal way
Synonyms: talk, speak, converse

"Nobody on this island ever heard of Darby," Silver said. "Shipmates, I never was feared of Flint in his life, and, by the powers, I'll face him dead. There's seven hundred thousand pound not a quarter of a mile from here."

But there was no sign of courage in his followers. Rather, there was growing fear.

"It's Flint's ghost!" one of the men cried. The terrified men would have run away if they had dared. But fear kept them together, and it kept them close by John, as if his daring helped them.

"His ghost? Well, maybe," Silver said. "But there's one thing not clear to me. There was an echo. Now, no man ever seen a spirit who had an echo." Silver suddenly roared. "By the powers, it was like Ben Gunn!"

"Ben Gunn!" the pirates cried. Their spirits returned and their natural color came back in their faces. Soon they were **chatting** together. Dead or alive, nobody minded Ben Gunn.

They moved forward, reaching the first of the tall trees, but those trees were the wrong ones. The second tree wasn't the right one, either. The third

CONSPICUOUS (kuhn <u>spik</u> yoo uhss) *adj.*
easily seen
Synonyms: obvious, noticeable

IMPRESS (im <u>press</u>) *v.* **-ing, -ed**
to have a strong effect on someone or
something
Synonyms: influence, strike

tree rose nearly two hundred feet into the air. It was **conspicuous** far to sea and might have been entered as a sailing mark upon the chart. It was only twenty or so yards away from us.

But it was not its size that now **impressed** my companions. It was the knowledge that seven hundred thousand pounds in gold lay somewhere buried below its spreading shadow!

Silver hobbled, grunting, on his crutch and at times turned to give me an angry look. He was close to the gold, and now all else had been forgotten. His promise and the doctor's warning were both things of the past. I could not doubt that he hoped to seize the treasure, find and board the *Hispaniola* under cover of night, cut every honest throat about that island, and sail away, as he had at first intended, with his riches.

"Now, mates, all together!" shouted Merry, and the pirates broke into a run toward the tree and the treasure.

Suddenly, not ten yards further, we saw them stop. A low cry arose. Silver moved even faster, digging away with the foot of his crutch like one

POSSESSED (poss <u>essd</u>) *adj.*
controlled by a supernatural being
Synonyms: bewitched, crazed

SPROUT (sprowt) *v.* **-ing, -ed**
to start to grow
Synonyms: bud, germinate

BRANDED (<u>brand</u> ed) *adj.*
marked with a burn from a hot iron
Synonyms: labeled, stamped

CACHE (cash) *n.*
a hiding place for money or goods
Synonyms: stash, reserve

possessed, and next moment he and I had come also to a dead halt.

Before us was a great hole, not very recent, for the sides had fallen in and grass had **sprouted** on the bottom. In the hole were the shaft of a pick axe broken in two and the boards of several packing-cases thrown around. On one of these boards I saw, **branded** with a hot iron, the name *Walrus* – the name of Flint's ship.

All was clear. The **cache** had been found and stolen! The seven hundred thousand pounds were gone!

REALIZE (ree uh lize) *v.* **-ing**, **-ed**
to become aware of
Synonyms: understand, comprehend

DISAPPOINTMENT (diss uh <u>point</u> ment) *n.*
a feeling of unhappiness because one did not
get what was expected
Synonyms: letdown, misfortune

CHAPTER 14

Each of the six men acted as though he had been struck. But with Silver the blow passed almost instantly. Every thought of his had been set on that money. But he kept his head and changed his plan before the others had had time to **realize** the **disappointment**.

"Jim," he whispered, "take that, and stand by for trouble." And he passed me a pistol.

At the same time, he began quietly moving northward, and in a few steps had put some land between us two and the other five. Then he

DISGUSTED (diss <u>gust</u> ed) *adj.*
feeling sick about something
    Synonyms: grossed out, repulsed

SCRAMBLE (<u>skram</u> buhl) *v.* **-ing**, **-ed**
to move quickly
    Synonyms: rush, scurry, clamber

looked at me and nodded. His looks were not quite friendly, and I was so **disgusted** at these constant changes that I could not help whispering, "So you've changed sides again."

There was no time left for him to answer me. The buccaneers, with oaths and cries, began to leap, one after another, into the pit and to dig with their fingers, throwing the boards aside as they did so. Morgan found a piece of gold and passed it hand to hand among the pirates.

"Two guineas!" roared Merry, shaking it at Silver. "That's all there is of your seven hundred thousand pounds, and you knew it all along, Silver!"

Everyone began to **scramble** out of the hole.

Well, there we stood, two on one side, five on the other, the pit between us.

Merry was raising his arm and his voice, and plainly meant to lead a charge. But just then – crack! crack! crack! Three musket shots flashed out of the thicket. Merry tumbled into the pit. Another man fell dead.

Before you could wink, Long John had fired two barrels of a pistol into the struggling Merry.

NICK (nik) *n.*
at the last possible moment
Synonyms: at the last moment

PROFOUNDLY (pruh <u>fownd</u> lee) *adv.*
in a deep way
Synonyms: greatly, extremely

WEARY (<u>wihr</u> ree) *adj.*
extremely tired
Synonyms: exhausted, fatigued

At the same moment, the doctor, Gray, and Ben Gunn joined us, with smoking muskets, from among the nutmeg trees.

"Forward!" cried the doctor. "We must keep 'em off the boats." And we set off at a great pace, through the bushes.

"Thank ye kindly, doctor," says Silver. "You came in at the **nick** of time!" He looked over at Ben Gunn. "So it's you, Ben Gunn!" he added.

"I'm Ben Gunn, I am," replied the marooned sailor.

The doctor related what had taken place. It was a story that **profoundly** interested Silver, and Ben Gunn was the hero from beginning to end.

Ben, in his long, lonely wanderings about the island, had found the skeleton. He had found the treasure and dug it up. He had carried the treasure on his back, in many **weary** journeys, from the foot of the tall pine to a cave he had on the two-pointed hill at the northeast corner of the island. And there it had stayed stored in safety since two months before the arrival of the *Hispaniola*.

When the doctor had gotten this secret from

INVOLVE (in <u>volvd</u>) *v.* **-ing, -ed**
    to be a part of
        Synonyms: include, connect

AMBUSH (am <u>bush</u>) *v.* **-ing, -ed**
    to attack from a hidden position
        Synonyms: surround, entrap

FORMER (<u>for</u> mur) *adj.*
    belonging to the past
        Synonyms: earlier, previous

SKIM (skim) *v.* **-ing, -ed**
    to move easily over or near a surface
        Synonyms: glide, flow

Ben on the afternoon of the attack, and when next morning he saw the ship deserted, he had gone to Silver. He had given Silver the chart, because it was now useless. He had also given him the stores of food, for Ben Gunn's cave was well supplied with goat meat.

That morning, finding that I would be **involved** in the disappointment he had prepared for the mutineers, Ben had started a new plan. He would leave the squire to guard the treasure at the cave. He knew I had to be rescued and that the best way to do that was to **ambush** the pirates. He remembered the <u>superstitions</u> of his **former** shipmates. He called out the voices and set out the skeleton as a compass to terrify them. This made ambushing them easier.

"Ah," said Silver, "it were fortunate for me that I had Hawkins here. You would have let old John be cut to bits, and you never given it a thought, doctor."

"Not a thought," replied Dr. Livesey cheerily.

By this time we had reached the boats. We were soon aboard, **skimming** swiftly over a

FLUSH (flussh) *v.* **-ing, -ed**
to redden in the face
Synonym: blush

VILLAIN (<u>vill</u> uhn) *n.*
a person who breaks the law or moral
standards
Synonyms: criminal, scoundrel

PROSECUTE (pross uh <u>kyoot</u>) *v.* **-ing, -ed**
to carry out a legal action against someone
Synonyms: charge, bring action against

smooth sea. Soon we were round the southeast corner of the island.

As we passed the two-pointed hill, we could see the black mouth of Ben Gunn's cave and a figure standing by it, leaning on a musket. It was the squire, and we waved a handkerchief and gave him three cheers, in which the voice of Silver joined as heartily as any.

Three miles farther, just inside the mouth of North Inlet, what should we meet but the *Hispaniola,* cruising by herself? Another anchor was got ready and dropped. We all pulled round again to Rum Cove, the nearest point for Ben Gunn's treasure house. Gray returned with the boat to the *Hispaniola,* where he was to pass the night on guard.

At the cove, the squire met us. To me he was polite and kind, saying nothing of my doings either in the way of blame or praise. At Silver's polite salute, he **flushed**.

"John Silver," he said, "you're a **villain**. I am told I am not to **prosecute** you. Well, then, I will not. But the dead men, sir, hang about your neck like stones."

GROSS (groze) *adj.*
complete, blatant
Synonym: flagrant

HEAP (heep) *n.*
a great amount, a lot
Synonyms: pile, mass

"Thank you kindly, sir," replied Long John.

"How dare you to thank me!" cried the squire. "It is a **gross** misuse of my duty! You should be hanged! Stand back."

We all entered the cave. It was a large, airy place, with a little spring and a pool of clear water and some plants. The floor was sand. Before a big fire lay Captain Smollett, and in a far corner, I saw great **heaps** of coin and bars of gold. That was Flint's treasure that we had come so far to seek and that had cost already the lives of seventeen men from the *Hispaniola*.

"Come in, Jim," said the captain. "Is that you, John Silver?"

What a supper I had that night, with all my friends around me. And what a meal it was, with Ben Gunn's salted goat. Never, I am sure, were people happier. And there was Silver, sitting back almost out of the firelight, but eating heartily, ready to spring forward when anything was wanted, even joining quietly in our laughter. He seemed to be the same polite seaman that he had been on our voyage out.

TRANSPORT (<u>tranz</u> port) *v.* **-ing**, **-ed**
to move from one place to another
Synonyms: carry, transfer

VARIED (<u>vair</u> eed) *adj.*
having many different kinds
Synonyms: assorted, mixed, diverse

BORED (bord) *adj.*
to have a hole made through something
Synonyms: drilled, pierced

The next morning we fell early to work. We needed to **transport** this great pile of gold a mile to the beach, and then three miles by boat to the *Hispaniola*. It was a great job for so small a number of workmen. The three pirates still upon the island did not greatly trouble us. A single sentry on the shoulder of the hill was enough to make us feel safe against any sudden ambush. Besides, we were sure they had had more than enough of fighting.

We kept working. Gray and Ben Gunn came and went with the boat, while the rest piled treasure on the beach. For my part, I was kept busy all day in the cave packing the money into bags.

It was a strange collection of treasure, so large and **varied**. I took great pleasure sorting all the pieces. There were English, French, Spanish, Portuguese, strange Oriental pieces stamped with what looked like wisps of string or bits of spider's web, round pieces and square pieces, and pieces **bored** through the middle, as if to wear them round your neck. There was nearly every kind of money in the world. Day after day this work went on. By the end of each day a fortune had been

SHRIEKING (shreek) *n.*

the sound of someone screaming wildly
Synonyms: yelling, shouting

APPROVAL (uh <u>prov</u> uhl) *n.*

acceptance of a plan or idea
Synonyms: support, permission

taken aboard, and we knew that there was another fortune waiting for us tomorrow. All this time we heard nothing of the three surviving mutineers.

At last, on the third night, the doctor and I were walking on the shoulder of the hill when, from out the darkness below, the wind brought us a noise between **shrieking** and singing. "Heaven forgive them," said the doctor; "That's the mutineers!"

Silver kept on trying to be friendly with all of us. Yet, I think, none treated him better than a dog, unless it was Ben Gunn, who was still terribly afraid of his old quartermaster, or myself.

Only once we heard a gunshot a great way off and supposed that it was the sound of the pirates hunting. A council was held, and it was decided that we must desert them on the island, to the huge glee of Ben Gunn, and with the strong **approval** of Gray. We left a good stock of powder and shot, the bulk of the salt goat, a few medicines, and some tools, clothing, a spare sail, some rope, and even a present of tobacco.

That was about our last doing on the island. Before that, we had got the treasure packed away.

REMAINDER (ruh <u>main</u> der) *n.*
the part which is left over
Synonyms: balance, excess

MERCIFUL (<u>mur</u> sih ful) *adj.*
having or showing kindness
Synonyms: gracious, compassionate

We also put on the ship enough water and the **remainder** of the goat meat. At last, on a fine morning, we pulled up our anchor and finally sailed out of North Inlet, our <u>colors</u> flying.

The three pirates must have been watching us. When we came through the narrows, we saw all three of them <u>kneeling</u> together on the sand, with their arms raised as if they were begging us for help. It went to all our hearts, I think, to leave them in that wretched state. But we could not risk another mutiny, and to take them home to be hanged would have been a cruel sort of kindness. The doctor hailed them and told them of the supplies we had left for them, and where they were to find them. But they kept calling us by name and begged us to be **merciful** and not leave them to die in such a place.

At last, seeing the ship still kept sailing, one of them pirates leapt to his feet with a cry, grabbed his musket to his shoulder, and sent a shot whistling through the main-sail.

After that, we kept under cover, and when next I looked out the pirates had disappeared. By

GULF (gulf) *n.*

an inlet of the sea almost surrounded land

Synonym: bay

CHARMING (<u>charm</u> ing) *adj.*

attractive or delightful

Synonyms: sweet, captivating

CONTRAST (<u>kon</u> trast) *n.*

a noticeable distinction between two things

Synonyms: difference, contradiction

noon, the highest rock of Treasure Island had sunk into the blue round of sea.

We were so short of men that everyone on board had to help out. The captain gave his orders from a bed, for he still needed peace and quiet. We sailed for the nearest port in Spanish America. We could not risk the voyage home without fresh hands.

It was just at sundown when we cast anchor in a most beautiful **gulf**, and were immediately surrounded by shore boats selling fruits and vegetables. Men offered to dive for bits of money. The sight of so many friendly faces, the taste of the tropical fruits, and above all the lights that began to shine in the town made a most **charming contrast** to our dark and bloody stay on the island.

The doctor and the squire, taking me along with them, went ashore to pass the early part of the night. Here they met the captain of an English ship and began to talk with him. They went on board his ship, and, in short, had so good a time that day was breaking when we came back to the *Hispaniola*.

Ben Gunn was on deck alone, and he made a

CONFESSION (kon <u>fesh</u> uhn) *n.*
a statement admitting to wrong doing
Synonyms: acknowledgment, declaration

PRESERVE (pri zurv) *v.* **-ing, -ed**
to keep safe from harm or injury
Synonyms: protect, maintain

RETIRE (ree <u>tire</u>) *v.* **-ing, -ed**
to stop working
Synonym: quit

confession. Silver was gone. Ben had helped him escape in a shore boat, and he had only done so to **preserve** our lives. He was sure our lives would have been lost if "that man with the one leg had stayed aboard." But this was not all. The cook had taken one of the sacks of coin, worth perhaps four hundred guineas, to help him on his wanderings.

No one was upset that Silver was gone. In fact, I think we were all pleased to be so cheaply rid of him.

Well, to make a long story short, we got a few hands on board, and we made a good cruise home. The *Hispaniola* reached Bristol just as the rescue ship was beginning to sail out to fetch us.

All of us had a good share of the treasure. We used it wisely or foolishly, according to our natures. And what became of all of us?

Captain Smollett has now **retired** from the sea. Gray not only saved his money, but he is now mate and part owner of a fine ship. He is also married besides, and he has become the father of a fine family. As for Ben Gunn, he got a thousand pounds, which he spent or lost in nineteen

NOTABLE (<u>note</u> uh buhl) *adj.*
worthy of notice
Synonyms: well-known, prominent

FORMIDABLE (<u>for</u> muh duh buhl) a*dj.*
causing fear
Synonyms: terrifying, dreadful

BOOMING (<u>boom</u> ing) *adj.*
making a loud, deep sound
Synonyms: blasting, roaring

days, for he was back begging for more money on the twentieth. Then he was given a house of his own, and he still lives there, and is a **notable** singer in church on Sundays.

Of Silver we have heard no more. That **formidable** <u>seafaring</u> man with one leg has at last gone clean out of my life. But I dare say he lives in comfort with his parrot, Captain Flint. It is to be hoped so, I suppose, for his chances of comfort in another world are very small.

<u>Oxen</u> and ropes would not bring me back again to that island. The worst dreams that ever I have are when I hear the surf **booming** about Treasure Island. Then, I start upright in bed with the sharp voice of Captain Flint still ringing in my ears: "Pieces of eight! Pieces of eight!"

RESOURCES

GLOSSARY

The following are words and terms that you are not likely to be tested on, but understanding them will enhance your appreciation of the text.

account book (uh <u>cownt</u> buk) *n.*
a book holding records of buying and selling and other money matters

admiral (<u>ad</u> muh ruhl) *n.*
a high-ranking officer in a navy

amphitheatre (<u>am</u> <u>fi</u> <u>thee</u> uh tur) *n.*
a large circular theater

antelope (<u>an</u> tell ope) *n.*
a fast-running animal that looks like a deer

barbecue (<u>barb</u> uh kwyu) *n.*
a charcoal grill used for cooking

berth (burth) *v.* **-ing**, **-ed**
to provide a place to sleep on a ship

biscuit (<u>biss</u> kit) *n.*
a kind of bread, genrally made as a small piece

blab (blab) *v.* **-ing**, **-ed**
gossip or chatter

bloodthirsty (<u>blud</u> thurst ee) *adj.*
eager to shed blood, murderous

boatswain (<u>bo</u> suhn) *n.*

the officer in charge of a ship's equipment

bonfire (<u>bon</u> fyre) *n.*

a large fire that is built outside

booty (<u>boo</u> tee) *n.*

an amount taken or seized illegally; loot

Bristol (<u>bris</u> tuhl) *n.*

city in southwestern England, well-known as a port

for sailing ships during the 1700s and 1800s

buccaneer (buh kuh <u>neer</u>) *n.*

a pirate

bulwark (<u>bull</u> work) *n.*

the part of a ship's sides that extend above the deck

cabin boy (<u>kab</u> ihn boy) *n.*

a young person hired to take care of a ship's officers

cable (<u>kabe</u> uhl) *n.*

a strong, heavy rope

chirp (<u>chirp</u>) *n.*

the high pitched sound made by an insect or bird

colors (<u>kull</u> uhrs) *n.*

flag, usually of a nation, ship, or military unit

compass (<u>kuhm</u> puhss) *n.*

a tool used to find geographic direction

cutlass (<u>cut</u> less) *n.*

a short sword with a curved blade, often used by sailors

coxswain (cocks ihn) *n.*

the person who steers a boat

Davy Jones (<u>Day</u> vee Jonz) *n.*

the evil spirit of the sea; in past times, "Davy Jones locker" was used to refer to the bottom of the sea or the burial site for drowned sailors

doubloon (dub <u>loon</u>) *n.*

a Spanish gold coin

echo (<u>ek</u> oh) *n.*

a sound that is heard after it has been reflected off a surface

farthing (<u>far</u> thing) *n.*

a coin equal to one quarter of an English penny

fathom (<u>fath</u> uhm) *n.*

a unit of length equal to six feet

figurehead (<u>fig</u> uhr hed) *n.*

a carving, usually of wood, set in the front, or bow, of a ship

fourpenny (<u>fore</u> pen ee) *n.*

a coin worth four pennies (pence)

galley (<u>gal</u> ee) *n.*

the cooking area or kitchen of a ship

gig (gig) *n.*

a light boat that can be either sailed or rowed

grog (grog) *n.*

a drink made of rum mixed with water

gulf (gulf) *n.*

a large area of sea partially surrounded by land

guinea (<u>gin</u> ee) *n.*

a British coin made from gold mined in West
Africa

hand (hand) *n.*

a person who engages in labor, especially the
member of a ship's crew

high-water mark (hi <u>waw</u> tuhr mahrk) *n.*

the level reached by the sea at high tide

Hispaniola (hiss pan ee <u>oh</u> lah) *n.*

during the days of the Spanish colonial empire,
the island on which are located the presnt-day
countries of Haiti and the Dominican Republic

human (<u>hyoo</u> man) *n.*

a person; man or woman

interior (in <u>tihr</u> ee ur) *n.*

the inside of a place

irons (<u>eye</u> urnz) *n.*

chains

kneel (neel) *v.* **-ing**, **-ed**

to bend so one has at least one knee on the ground

lather (<u>lath</u> uhr) *n.*

a foamy substance made by mixing soap and
water

latitude (<u>lat</u> uh tood) *n.*

the position of a place measured in degrees from
the equator

longitude (<u>lon</u> juh tood) *n.* **-ing**, **-ed**

the position of a place measured in degrees going
east or west from the Prime Meridian, which is
an imaginary line that runs through Greenwich,
England

loophole (<u>loop</u> hole) *v.*

to make small holes, usually to see or shoot
through

magistrate (<u>maj</u> uh strait) *n.*

a local official sometimes acting as a judge

mainmast (<u>mane</u> mast) *n.*

the central, tallest mast on a sailing ship

mainsail (<u>mane</u> sil) *n.*

the principal sail of a sailing ship

medical (<u>med</u> uh kuhl) *adj.*

relating to the treatment of an injury of illness

midday (<u>mid</u> day) *n.*

in the middle of the day or the afternoon

musket (<u>muss</u> ket) *n.*

a light gun carried by infantry that is fired
from the shoulder

musket balls (<u>muss</u> ket balz) *n.*

the round, lead bullets shot from a musket

muzzle (<u>muhzz</u> uhl) *n.*

the open end of a gun barrel

nay (nay) *adv.*

no

oilcloth (<u>oyl</u> clawth) *n.*

a fabric that has been treated with oil on one
side to make it waterproof

overboard (<u>oh</u> vur bord) *adv.*

over the edge of the ship and into the ocean

ox (oks) *n.*

an adult bull

pieces of eight (<u>pees</u> uhs uv ate) *n.*

Spanish gold coins

pistol (<u>piss</u> tuhl) *n.*

a small gun that can be held and fired with one hand

plank (plank) *n.*

a long, flat piece of wood placed on the edge of a ship, like a diving board, over the ocean; to "walk the plank" means to be forced to walk along it until one falls into the ocean

pound (pownd) *n.*

the basic unit of English money

powder horn (<u>pow</u> duhr horn) *n.*

an object used to hold gunpowder, often made from the horn of an ox

quarterdeck (<u>kwar</u> tuhr dek) *n.*

the part, at the back or stern of a ship, reserved for use by the captain

quartermaster (<u>kwar</u> tuhr mast uhr) *n.*

the officer in charge of supplies

regiment (<u>rej</u> uh ment) *n.*

    a military group or unit

saber (<u>say</u> bur) n.

    a short, heavy sword with a single cutting edge

schooner (<u>skoo</u> nuhr) *n.*

    a sailing ship with two or more masts

seafaring (<u>see</u> fair ing) *adj.*

    relating to the sea or to being a sailor

sheath (sheeth) *n.*

    a close fitting cover for a knife

shiver my timbers (<u>shiv</u> uhr my <u>tim</u> buhrz) *exclam.*

    an expression of surprise that refers to how
    the masts of a ship can suddenly split when a
    ship runs aground or is struck by lightning or a
    cannon ball

squire (sqwire) *n.*

    an English country gentleman, often someone
    who owns the most land in a certain area

statue (<u>stach</u> oo) *n.*

    a three-dimensional likeness of a human or
    animal modeled with a material such as stone,
    clay, or bronze.

superstition (<u>soo</u> pur <u>sti</u> shun) *n.*

a belief in signs connected to magic or ancient
ideas

tattooed (ta <u>tood</u>) *adj.*

marked with a permanent design made by using
needles to put color under the skin

telescope (<u>tel</u> uh scope) *n.*

an instrument that makes distant objects look
bigger

thigh (thi) *n.*

the part of the leg between the hip and the knee

tiller (<u>til</u> uhr) *n.*

a long, wooden steering piece for a boat or ship

trigger (<u>trigg</u> ur) *n.*

the part of a gun you pull with your finger to fire
the weapon

vise (vice) *n.*

a tool that holds something firmly in place so it
can be worked on vise

volunteer (<u>vol</u> uhn tighr) *n.*

a person who does something willingly

watch (wach) *n.*

a work crew given a job for a specific period of time

BOOK REPORT

Students are often asked to write book reports about the books they read. The key to writing a good report is to organize your ideas before you start writing. Use the following questions to organize your ideas for a book report about *Treasure Island.*

1. What is the title?
2. Who is the author? What do you know about him?
3. When and where does the story take place?
4. Who is the main character of the book?
5. What happens to this person during the story? What is this person like at the beginning? And at the end? What problems does this person face? How does this person solve them?
6. Who are the other important characters? What are they like? What happens to them?
7. What do you think is the main theme or idea of the book?
8. What is the main thing you learned from this book?
9. What would you tell a friend about this book if he or she asked you about it?

DISCUSSION QUESTIONS

Here are several questions to think about and to discuss with classmates and other people who have read Robert Louis Stevenson's *Treasure Island*:

1. Jim Hawkins meets a number of astonishing characters during his adventure. Which do you think he will remember the most? Why?

2. Why do you think Jim Hawkins is so willing to abandon his home and set off to sea?

3. Long John Silver is considered one of the classic "villains" of literature. Do you think Silver is an entirely evil character? Why or why not?

4. Jim and his friends manage to triumph over the pirates in spite of overwhelming odds. Does this seem realistic or possible to you? Why or why not?

5. *Treasure Island* has been considered both a book for adults and a book for children. Which do you think it is? Why?